Noel's Miracle

G. Phillip Ungricht

Preface

In an age of cynicism, I wanted to write a book which would cause the reader to put aside the natural skepticism which is so prevalent in our society today, and embrace a reason for living. Jesus Christ should be synonymous with Christmas, but the commercial element of the season seems to have pushed Christ aside. I hope with *Noel's Miracle* one can move his or her spirit closer to the well of happiness by remembering Jesus Christ, who is the true "reason for the season." This book illustrates the power of Christmas when holiday traditions center around love, family, and an understanding of Jesus Christ's gift to the world. It transforms mere words into lasting Christmas memories.

I owe a great deal of thanks to my mother, Elva, and my grandmother, Vera, who, at a very early age, instilled within me a deep love of Christmas. Without them, there would have been no story to write. My grandfather, Albert (who everybody called "Dad"), to me was the greatest storyteller in the world. He became the inspiration for the character Noel in this book. My wife, Mollie, with her unwavering faith and confidence, provided me with the motivation to write, and without her encouragement, this book would have never been completed. And last of all, to my children: Adrian, Brynn, George, and Hillary, this book is a reminder of all things important in life and where your priorities need to be.

Chapter 1

It was cold. In fact, it was too cold. The big lake was living up to its reputation and the soft, fluffy, white flakes of snow falling heavily from the sky didn't temper its fury one bit. Many years had passed since the homes surrounding Lake Michigan had been battered by such a storm. It seemed to have everyone holed up. Everyone, that is, except a jolly, eighty-year old man with a beautiful head of white hair and a love of December snowstorms, Noel Trudeau.

He had started a fire when he climbed out of bed first thing in the morning, trying to initiate the ambience of the holiday season. The warm fire succored his comfortable home as he sat at his kitchen table finishing the last bites of hot cakes smothered in maple syrup, a couple of strips of bacon, and a cup of hot cocoa.

Just off to the side of the kitchen table was a maze of tangled Christmas lights and decorations he had pulled out from under the stairway earlier that morning. Every year when he took them out he cursed himself for just dumping them into boxes and shoving them away the previous year. But he hated to take them down. It depressed him. Christmas just didn't last long enough. So with a potpourri of cinnamon and cloves simmering on the stove and Christmas carols playing on his stereo, he carefully worked through the jumbled mess with a happy, humble smile on his weathered lips.

He rose from the table as if prompted by a higher power and moved over to an old, patched wooden orange crate. He reached into the ancient crate and gently pulled out the well-worn pieces of an antique nativity set. Carrying the nativity into the living room, he reflected on the special memory of each piece and positioned the set in perfect spacing on an old Queen Anne table covered with angel hair next to the fireplace. It was something he had done many, many times before.

He pondered a few extra moments over the final piece of the nativity and then, with his sight blurred from the tears formed beneath his eyes, he set the cherubic Christ child among the other hand-carved pieces.

"Perfect!" he exclaimed as a large grin spread over his face.

"Now for the lights outside."

Moving back into the kitchen, he gazed out at the deepening snow through the compact window above the sink. Seeing that the storm had slackened off from the heavy blizzard which had blasted earlier in the morning, he shifted over to the mud room where he grabbed his old, faithful red and black woolen coat and matching hat with ear flaps. They were worn in several places, but were like old friends, welcome and comfortable. Pulling the hat onto his head, he bent the flaps down to cover his ears and escaped out into the blowing snow, carrying a large box of lights in his arms. Bringing them around to the front yard, he hummed the tune to "It's Beginning to Look a Lot Like Christmas."

Setting the box on the front porch, he took a strand of lights and carefully laid them on the ground in front of his house and untangled them. Then it was back to the box where he grabbed another strand and continued the process until the lights were laid out upon the ground exactly like they would hang on the roof of his home.

Breathing heavily, he trudged back through the fallen snow to the open single-stall garage. Inside was an old-fashioned wooden ladder hung from hooks on the side of the garage wall. Lifting the ladder, he lugged it around to the front of his house where he propped its braces open by the corner eave.

Out of breath, he crouched his head close to his chest, seeking protection from the blowing wind, and climbed up the steps of the ladder. Reaching high above his head, he fastened one end of the strand of lights to the small cup hook embedded in the wooden cornice of his home.

He threaded the strand of lights through each appropriately placed hook along the edge of the roof. When he could reach no further, he fastened the last light into its assigned cup hook and then climbed down and moved the ladder. Repeating the process again and again, he worked the lights up and around the small gable covering the entryway and then paused to rest one more time. With a deep gasp, he filled his lungs and grabbed the end of the next string of lights, climbed up the rungs, and reached for the end of the strand already dangling from the porch gable. Grasping the swinging end, he plunged the prongs of the new set into their proper place. Suddenly, a sharp, piercing pain drove deep into his back and threw him into the steps of the ladder. Shards of white light flashed back and forth through his head as the pain from his back coursed through his entire body. Wildly, he clutched his arms around the ladder and clung to the rungs, clamoring for air. The intense pain made it impossible to suck any oxygen into his lungs, but an errant scream escaped his lips as unconsciousness gripped the old man and he crumpled from the ladder onto the frozen ground with a deep, dense thud.

Laying motionless on the ground, the heavenly snow began to cover the huddled red and black mass of the fallen elderly man, leaving his precious Christmas decorating incomplete.

Chapter 2

The University Hospital had opened eight months ago as a joint, state-of-the-art teaching facility for Northwestern University and the University of Chicago. It possessed the most efficient emergency room in the entire state, run by the youngest director of emergency medical services, thirty-five-year old Dr. Katarina Stone. However, her appointment had not surprised the hospital administrator, Logan Stone. He had met and married Katarina five years ago, right after she was assigned to St. Bonaventure, and over the past five years he had become accustomed to her drive. Focused was the word he used to describe her, but consumed was more precise.

She had been preparing for this assignment ever since she had watched her mother, Sabrina, and her twin sister, Kolina, die on adjoining gurneys in an understaffed emergency room following an automobile accident thirty years ago. Her father, Donald Bettweiser, was a hard-working railroad engineer and for a while he tried to raise his remaining daughter alone. However, he couldn't cope with the memories of his home and his life without his wife, and he began spending more and more time away from home. The most difficult decision of his life was placing Kat in the custody of the state, where she was shuffled thereafter from foster home to foster home. Donald's abandonment devastated Kat, and she rebelled every chance she could. Her rebellion grew worse and worse over the next seven years until she eventually ran away. After that, she was placed into a home for wayward teenagers where she stayed until she went to college.

It was during these high school years that she learned to compete, and she had been competing ever since. In college, she earned her way to the top of her class at George Washington University and when she filled her fellowship, those who worked with her agreed she was the finest doctor they had ever seen in the emergency program. It was with this same intense desire that she carried out her first directorship. This morning was no different.

Striding into the spotless, antiseptic corridor of the ER, she called out, "Where is everybody?"

"Everyone's here, Dr. Stone," answered Phil Baker, one of several emergency room orderlies.

"That's funny, Phil. I don't see anyone here but you."

"They're here, alright. They're either getting coffee, checking on patients, or looking for some Christmas decorations, but I've seen everyone this morning."

"My nurses too?"

"Yeah! They're trying to find some Christmas music in the locker room. I told them I would keep an eye on everything while they checked."

"Well, play time is over. You get everyone down here now. The snow outside is going to wreak havoc and it's all going to land right here. I can feel it," she reproached.

"No problem, Dr. Stone. I'm on my way," he replied as he hustled down the hall.

Kat turned as she heard a noisy group of nurses bustling behind her. Just as she was about to rebuke them, the dispatch radio crackled behind the ER nurses' station.

"University Hospital, this is emergency unit two. Come in, please."

Scrambling behind the counter, Sarah White, a sparkling, vivacious young woman, pressed the communications button on the radio and answered, "This is University Hospital. Unit two come in."

"University Hospital, this is unit two. We have casualties from a multiple car accident on I-94. It's really a mess out here. We'll bring you all you can handle and divert the rest to St. Francis. If we have to, we'll send the kids down to Children's Memorial."

"Unit two, what is the seriousness of the injuries?"

"At least one is dead and several others are critically injured. This accident is a bad one, at least thirty to forty cars. Right now, we're bringing in a head injury, a back injury, and another with severe lacerations. Should be there in about seven to ten minutes."

"Okay, unit two. We'll be ready. See you in seven."

Kat was organizing in her mind the whole time Sarah was talking to the emergency unit and immediately started shouting out orders when Sarah finished, "Phil, prep every room and make sure they're ready. Dan, Gary, and Trish, take the patients as they come, in rooms two, three, and four. I'll triage with Sarah until we're swamped, then I'll take what I can in room one."

Before she finished her commands, everyone in the ER had moved off in a flurry of activity. In what seemed like seconds instead of minutes, the power doors of the ER entryway slid open and the paramedics rushed in with filled gurneys.

"We have a head and neck injury with lacerations about the face and chest. Pulse is rapid. Blood pressure 90 over 40 and we've started an IV drip."

In one quick motion, Katarina flew into action. Each medical person performed like a precise cog in a well-oiled machine. Doctors moved from patient to patient, caring for each with utmost dignity, as they treated every trauma. The nurses wove in and out with expert precision, as the orderlies cleaned the used rooms and transported the treated patients to their new holding facilities. Minutes turned into hours as the exhausted emergency personnel continued to bring new patients into the ER, where the doctors and nurses were starting to show signs of weariness.

"Dan, let Dana close there. I need you over here now," Kat exclaimed.

Daniel Smoot, a middle-aged, balding doctor who was usually quite pleasant, was about to joust back, but thought better of it. He hurried over to her side while he tore the used latex gloves from his hands, discarded them, and stuffed his hands into new, clean ones. As he stepped next to Kat's side, Sarah clamored into the cramped examination room and yelled, "Dr. Stone, we need you in one. Gold Cross just brought us someone almost frozen to death."

Kat spun around immediately and followed, calling as she ran, "What have we got, Sarah?"

"It's an elderly man. The paramedics found him in his front yard covered with snow. They don't even know how long he was out there. He was already laying on the ground when someone driving by saw him and called 911."

As Kat entered the small room, she spoke to the three nurses surrounding the patient, "Let's get his clothes off and start an IV, but warm the fluids first.

Sarah, grab some heated blankets and start warming his extremities. We've got to elevate his temperature."

Kat moved over to the bed after issuing instructions and began to check the patient. Looking closely at him, a strange stab of recognition ripped through her entire being, sending shock waves reverberating off the walls of her mind. Stepping back, she shook her head and tried to gain her professional composure.

As she stared blindly into the patient's face, she couldn't confirm the recognition so she shouted, "Amanda, did you take his temperature?"

Before she could answer, Dana Morgan yelled out as she began CPR, "Code blue! Code blue! Grab a crash cart, stat."

Kat shoved Dana out of the way, grabbed the shirt they were trying to remove, and ripped it open, exposing the bare chest of the old man.

"Give me the paddles!" Kat shouted.

Immediately Sarah handed her the paddles from the crash cart now in position and screamed, "Clear!"

The body of the elderly man bounced off the gurney a few inches as the electric shock ripped through his torso, but his heart didn't respond.

Without pause, Kat cried, "Repeat, clear!" Again the body jumped off the gurney responding to the jolt of electricity, but again the heart did not start beating.

With tension mounting among the workers in the small examination room faster than the snow falling outside, Kat hollered above the drone, "Sarah, give me 10 milligrams of epinephrine and push, stat!"

Without delay, a syringe filled with the requested drug was slapped into her hand. Pushing the elongated needle into the exposed vein, she administered the medication and cried, "Dana, double the jouwls on the paddles and everybody clear."

This time the body jerked severely in reaction to the shock, as it bounced on the gurney.

"We have a beat," Sarah triumphantly announced.

"Okay, give me 80 milligrams of lidocaine and start a lidocaine drip," Kat demanded. She dropped the paddles and began massaging the chest until Sarah handed her a syringe filled with lidocaine.

While Kat dispensed the lidocaine, Julie called out, "His blood pressure is falling."

"Then add another IV with a dopamine drip."

Pushing back from the gurney, Katarina watched the nurses as they worked at warming the patient. Relieved, Amanda announced, "The temperature is 94 degrees and rising."

Almost as an afterthought, Kat announced, "He'll make it." Then she moved away from the bustle surrounding the unknown patient, but as she did, the strange and disturbing pang of recognition returned.

Chapter 3

It had been a long, arduous day and Kat was in no mood for the banter she discovered when she walked into Noel Trudeau's room.

"Come on, Sarah, won't you get it for me?" he begged.

"I won't have time tonight, Noel. Maybe one of the other nurses can go get it for you," she replied.

Picking up his chart, Kat interrupted the dialogue and asked, "Get what?"

Sarah turned to look at who had joined them and said, "I'm sorry, Dr. Stone. I didn't see you come in."

"That didn't answer my question, Sarah. Get what?"

Noel answered for her. "My precious nativity. Sarah tells me I've got to stay in the hospital for a while. I really can't be without my nativity during this season."

Immediately, Kat was overwhelmed with a strange familiarity. She suggested, "Can't you pick it up on your way home, Sarah?"

"I'm not going home tonight, Dr. Stone. Matthew is taking me to a Bulls game. He's picking me up here at the hospital."

Noel interjected, "Could you pick it up for me, Dr. Stone?"

"I don't think so," she replied. Before she could explain further, he pleaded, "Please, Dr. Stone. You're my last hope."

The intensity of the strange feeling grew as she turned and took the piece of paper he was holding with the address of his house. "Very well. I'll pick it up on my way home. How far away is your home from here, anyway?"

"Not very far, Dr. Stone. It's just over by the lake. I've written down the directions and the house should be open."

She looked over the instructions and stuffed the paper into the pocket of her lab coat. As she left the room, she called out, "Sarah, make sure Mr. Trudeau gets his meds before you go."

Once outside Noel's room, Kat made her way to her office. As she approached her desk, she found a stack of reports which had to be completed before she went home. She sat down and began sifting through the papers. Minutes turned into hours. While she pored over a report, the door to her office flew open and in burst her husband.

"Burning the midnight oil?" he asked.

"Not any more than you are, my dear."

"Well, it's time to go home. Can you wrap things up so we can leave?" he asked.

"Sure, but I need to make a stop on the way home."

"No problem. Where do you need to stop?"

"I'll tell you in the car. Why don't you pull it around and pick me up outside the front entrance? I'll just gather a few things to take with me, then I'll check out and be down in a few minutes."

"Don't be too long. You're on call tonight and after the day you've had, you need to get some sleep," he tenderly added.

"Don't remind me. But if you don't leave now, I'll be down before you are," she responded, poking her pen in mock anger into his side.

Spinning around in her chair, she gathered the reports scattered over her desk and stuffed them into her briefcase. She picked up her coat, switched the light off, and locked the door behind her. Walking down the polished hallway, she stopped to check the lightly falling snow out the window of the breeze way connecting the two buildings. Although it had tapered off from the heavy blanket already left, intermittent flurries lightened the night sky.

Instantly, she was mesmerized by the falling snow. Then that same unusual sensation she had felt earlier in the ER swept over her again. Knowing Logan was downstairs waiting, she started towards the exit.

But something more powerful constrained her to stop and turn back towards this strange man.

Room 1225 was in the A wing of the hospital, the same wing as the emergency room and Kat's office. It was on the second floor which was just up one floor from where she stood. Justifying the closeness, she immediately went there and slipped into the room. The eery silence of the private hospital room was punctuated by the persistent beep of the machines connected to the sleeping patient, Noel Trudeau. Kat checked the heart monitor and the IV and found everything normal. That convinced her the sensation was nothing more than a nuisance. Just before she left, she stopped at the foot of the bed and gazed at the sleeping man. Picking up his chart from its holder, she stared at the name and whispered to herself, "Noel Trudeau! Who are you and why do I think I know you?" Unable to grasp the answers, she placed the chart back into its holder and slipped out of the room where she caught the elevator down to her waiting husband in the car.

"You said you were going to hurry," he stated as she slid onto the cold leather seat beside him.

"I was, but I had this feeling something was wrong with a patient, so I stopped in briefly to check on him before I came down."

"What patient was that?" he asked as he pulled away from the hospital entrance and onto the street, negotiating the snow-packed roads.

"He's the elderly man I admitted today . . . the one who almost froze to death."

"Is he going to make it?"

"I think so. All of his signs are stable, but I've been getting this feeling all afternoon."

"What feeling is that?" asked Logan.

"You're not going to believe me if I tell you."

"Try me."

"It's strange. It's like I know this man from somewhere. In fact, when I first looked at him, I thought he was my Dad. Crazy, huh?" she explained, her dark brown eyes penetrating his reflective gaze.

"Oh, I don't know. What made you think that?"

"Beats me. It just sort of swept over me, but I don't think I've ever met that man before in my life. It's just that every time I look at him or talk to him, I get this overwhelming sensation of familiarity."

"So, you have talked to him?"

"Yes."

"Well, did you ask him?"

"No! I couldn't just blurt out something like that. But I did do something else."

"What's that?"

"I promised him I would go to his house and pick up something for him."

"You've got to be kidding."

"I'm not kidding. He expects me to bring it to him tomorrow."

21

Logan turned his head slightly and pondered Kat's plans away from her direct gaze. He was confused by her out-of-character behavior. Kat had periodically searched for her father ever since they were married, but she never allowed it to interfere with her job. She always kept her job separate from everything else. It was placed on a pedestal and nothing, but nothing, interfered with it. However, sneaking a glance at her, he could see in her eyes that it was better not to push this situation anymore. So, he shook his head and asked, "Do you have directions to this man's house?"

"Yes. It's not that far. He lives in Evanston, over by the beach, about three miles away. It shouldn't take long. I'll just slip in, look around, pick it up, and slip out."

"How are you going to get in?"

"He said it should be open."

"I hope so."

His train of thought was cut off by a harsh stare so he snickered, causing his lips to turn into the big, broad grin he was famous for, as he asked, "What's so important in, what's his name?"

"Noel. Noel Trudeau."

"What's so important in Noel's house, that it couldn't wait until a family member brought it to him?"

"I'm not going to tell you if you're going to be so flippant," she censured as she pulled the written instructions to Noel's house out of her pocket and read them to Logan.

"Turn right at the corner and work your way over to Front Street. Turn left on Front Street and go north through three traffic lights, where you'll turn left again onto Victoria Street. His house will be the fourth house up on the right. A small, yellow bungalow."

"Okay, okay, I promise not to laugh. I just want to know what is so important that it would cause you to get overly involved with a patient?"

Looking at her husband, trying to decide whether or not to tell him, she finally answered, "A Christmas nativity set."

Expecting further explanation, Logan waited in silence, baffled by the simple revelation. When it didn't come, he asked, "Is that it? A nativity set? I was thinking it would be something more grandiose."

"So was I, but it wasn't. For whatever reason, this nativity is very important to him. He was almost pleading when he asked me to get it and then that feeling came over me and I just couldn't refuse!"

"Hey, it's okay with me. It just seems a little strange, that's all."

"It is strange and that's what bothers me. I'm sure I've never met him before, but I can't shake this feeling. It hit me again just before I left and that's why I stopped by his room before I came down. What do you think it is?" she pleaded, hoping Logan had the answer.

"I think you're exhausted and need a break . . ."

Interrupting him mid sentence, but not wanting to start an argument, she stated, "Not that again, Logan. I don't want to discuss vacation plans right now. I want to pick up the old nativity and get home. I am exhausted and I have to get some rest."

Before he could retaliate, Kat almost shouted out, "There it is! It's that small house on the right."

Logan pulled the car over to the curb and slid to a stop in the heavy snow. Getting out, he walked around to open the door for his wife. Before he could get there, she had already flung the door open wide and was slipping and sliding her way up to the front door.

While she stopped at the porch to bang the snow off of her shoes, Logan caught up and stomped his feet as well. He opened the painted wooden door bearing a well-worn Christmas wreath. As the old door creaked on its hinges, the curious couple quickly brushed their wet feet on a tattered yuletide welcome mat and entered the quaint home.

"Listen, Kat. It's Christmas music. I wonder why it's still playing? Maybe it's stuck. We'd better find it and turn it off."

"Okay, but I'm not going to go nosing around the house of some old man I've just met. You search for the music and I'll find the nativity," she said.

"All right, but you don't need to be so grumpy."

"I'm not grumpy. I just don't like rummaging through other people's stuff."

"Don't worry. I'll turn off the music while you grab the nativity," he called as he started looking for the source of the carols.

Kat spun on her heel and walked into the living room, where the fresh scent of pine filtered through the cramped room from a sparsely decorated tree in front of the window. An inexplicable urge to look at everything in the house fell over her as she stopped and faced the front wall where she saw the cold, burned-out ashes from the fire Noel had started earlier in the day. Her eyes were drawn to several pictures displayed with precision on the mantel over the fireplace. Hope of finding someone she knew prompted her to take a closer look.

Picking up each picture individually, she examined them to see if she recognized someone. In one picture, she could identify a younger Noel with jet black hair, his arm wrapped around a beautiful girl with long auburn hair. Obviously his wife, she thought, but no recognition came to her. In another photo, she saw a young couple with three small children posing for the camera in front of the Grand Canyon. A startling resemblance between the woman in the photograph and the man she was treating caught her attention. However, it didn't help her place them in her memory. Putting the picture back on the mantel, her rever-

ie was broken when Logan called out from the hallway, "Kat, you've got to come and see this! I haven't
seen one of these in years."

Moving quickly into the hallway, she gazed into
the open bay of the console Logan was pointing at
and asked, "What am I supposed to be seeing
here?"

"The tape player," he explained, a little exasperated that she hadn't seen it immediately.

"And what's so special about a tape player?"

"It's not just a tape player, Kat. It's an eight-track
tape player, the machine that revolutionized the
music world when we were teenagers. That's why
the music has been playing all day. It just goes from
one track to another and then repeats itself."

"I've never seen one of those before. It must have
been before my time," she chided good-naturedly.

"Right, dear. Did you find what you came for?"

"Not yet, but I've found some interesting pictures.
Logan, look around. It's like a step back in time. I
haven't seen Christmas ornaments like those on his
tree since I was a child and Mom was alive."

"It's nostalgic, all right. You know, it's hard to imagine that people don't change with the times. I mean,
look at us. Our lives are constantly changing and
sometimes they can't change fast enough," Logan
explained. Together they walked arm in arm back
into the living room.

"It even smells like another era," she noticed.

"Yeah, like a shop right out of Dickens' *Christmas Carol.*"

"I don't know about that, but it's unbelievably comfortable," she added, walking off to examine the decorated Christmas tree more closely.

For some unknown reason, Kat was at home in this strange man's house. She was content looking around at all of the outdated surroundings and then she spied the nativity set and said, "There it is, Logan, on that table next to the fireplace. I was so caught up in looking at the pictures on the mantel that I overlooked the purpose of our visit. As your father would say, if it was a snake it would have bit me."

"That's bitten, dear," he corrected.

"For you and me and any other educated person, it's bitten, but for your dad it's bit," she chuckled.

Disturbed about Kat's comfort, Logan requested, "Let's pack it up and get out of here. I don't know what it is, but something just doesn't feel right to me."

"Okay, go ahead, but let me take one last look around, then I'll be ready to join you," she said to her husband as he walked to the front door and headed for the car. As quickly as she could, she packed up the treasured nativity for her patient. While she was packing, a compassionate glow filled her otherwise hard heart, prompting an unexpected swell of emotions to well up inside. Fighting back this unforeseen surge of sentiment, she moved very methodically around the outmoded room.

Just before she bid the humble habitat goodbye, she stopped and paused at the front door, locked it, and savored the feelings she hadn't felt since her mother had passed away. Hearing Logan honk the horn signaling her to come on, she closed the door and headed for the waiting car. Out in the storm again, she felt the need to protect what she had taken. So, she tucked the small, cherished package inside her coat close to her breast and braced for the slippery trip to the car.

Chapter 4

The loud blast of the ringing telephone shattered the peaceful silence of the cold, dark night. Rolling over on her side, Katarina fumbled with the blaring phone on her Chippendale night stand. Finally, after the fourth ring, she wrestled the phone from its base and piloted it to her ear. Gathering her wits, she breathed into the phone, "Hello! Yes . . . I'm on my way."

Placing the telephone back in its cradle, she sat on the edge of the bed trying to shed the cobwebs which remained from her deep slumber.

Logan shifted his body over and groggily asked, "Hospital call?"

Wriggling around to face him, she placed her hand on his shoulder and answered, "Yes. There's been an apartment fire and patients are backing up in the ER. Go back to sleep and I'll just slip out quietly."

"Will you be back before I leave for work?"

"I don't think so. It's three-thirty now and I seriously doubt I'll finish in time to come back home. I'll just stay at the hospital and catch up with you later," she said as she shivered from the cold, her body adjusting to being out from under the warm goose down comforter.

Remembering what the roads were like the night before, Logan suggested, "I'm sure it's awful out there. Take the Land Rover and I'll drive the Saab, but make sure you put it in four-wheel drive. After yesterday, you'll need all the traction you can get at this time of the morning. I'll bet the snow has been coming down all night."

By the time he finished his admonition, Kat was dressed and ready to walk out the door. She stopped before she left, wrapped a blue and green plaid scarf around her neck, stuffed the ends inside her navy blue wool coat, and called out, "I will. Now go back to sleep and I'll see you later at the hospital. Love you."

"I love you, too. Be careful," he added from under his pillow, where he had buried his head to go back to sleep. Then she was gone out of the bedroom, down the stairs, in the garage, and into the waiting automobile.

The bitterly cold night air had crusted the snow and the light wind had polished the ice-packed streets to a hazardous glare. Navigating the slick roads proved difficult, but the traction generated by the four-wheel drive vehicle delivered Kat to the hospital only fifteen minutes later than usual. Within seconds after she arrived, she hustled into the ER and demanded, "Stephanie, what's our condition here and where am I needed most?"

Stephanie Hickam, a chunky, middle-aged, single mother working graveyards as the head nurse in ER, answered, "Dr. Stone, take room four. They're piled up all over. Geoff was going to take it, but I need him in two."

"Got it, Steph," she answered as she pulled on a pair of latex gloves. Making her way through the nurses surrounding the patient in room four, she peered over the cindered body of a small child. Without notice, a wave of emotion crashed over her, wrenching at her heart and causing her body to shudder. Staring up from the gurney straight at her was the charred face of what looked like a six- or seven-year old.

Dreaded memories flashed through Kat's mind like a strobe. First was the memory of kneeling beside the bruised little body of her bunk mate, Cindy, after she had been thrown by their foster father. She had tried to ease Cindy's pain by wiping a cold cloth over her forehead, but nothing seemed to work, so she had just cradled her. Then she remembered an experience when she was a young intern at Beth Israel Hospital. She had been on staff when a small child was admitted for injuries resulting from an automobile accident. The boy was so badly injured that Kat couldn't handle it. No matter how hard she tried, all she could see was the lifeless body of her sister, Kolina, laying there on the gurney. She had grabbed another intern, pushed him toward the gurney, and fled from the ER, unable to cope. She understood it when adults got hurt. It was almost always the result of their own decisions. But children got hurt without having had any control. They were so helpless and just seemed to suffer so.

Grabbing the side rail of the little burn victim's gurney, Kat gathered control and forced the hated memories away. She choked back tears and charged, "Get fluids with a morphine drip hooked up, stat. Intubate her with a nasal tracheal intubation so she can breathe and let's hope there's no serious injury to the lungs from the smoke." Pausing for only a moment, she continued, "These facial burns look the worst. She probably covered her head with something like a blanket to protect herself from the flames and when it caught fire, well, you can see the results. Terry, give me a scalpel and some forceps. We need to debride the burned skin. Let's start around the eyes and work out from there."

Instantly, the three nurses at the bedside reacted to Dr. Stone's instructions. Placing their gloved hands on the child, they shifted her on the gurney, making her face accessible. As Tina moved the child's scorched head to try to intubate her, a small, helpless whimper escaped the tiny blistered lips.

The child's audible grief caused Kat to shout, "Have we got the morphine going?"

"Yes, Doctor. It should kick in any second."

"It better. This poor kid has suffered enough," she warned.

With meticulous precision and tender concern, the skilled hands of Doctor Stone contended with the destroyed tissue as they carefully removed the charred skin. After finishing the debriding around the eyes, she swiftly moved to the top of the child's head where the hair had been burned away. Her hands moved quickly and deftly around to the right side of the head, where the small ear had been destroyed. From the right ear she moved to the middle of the face, where all that remained of the child's nose were two holes in the middle of a bloody mass of incinerated flesh. As she worked her way down the small neck to the chest and arms of the youngster, the smell became overwhelming. Stifling her urge to vomit, she observed the severity of the burns that decreased as she moved further down the body.

"Her pajamas must have been nonflammable, because they provided some protection. It looks like the body burns have been limited to second degree."

When the child's petite hands were debrided, Kat directed, "Terry, wash what you can with a betadine solution and then, Tina, get some silvadene to cover the wounds. We don't want any infection setting in.

When you're finished, get her down to X-ray and see if there is any damage to her lungs, but keep her on the respirator until she regains consciousness, just as a precaution. I can't hear anything over the scope, but I want to make sure."

With gentle swathes, Terry began washing the wounds and then Tina applied the topical antibiotic ordered by Dr. Stone.

Stepping away from the bedside, Kat stretched while she watched the nurses finish the treatment. Walking into the small room, Stephanie placed her hand on Kat's shoulder and asked, "Is she going to make it, Doctor?"

Turning and looking at Stephanie with hollow, emotionless eyes, she responded with callous indifference, "I think so, Steph, but it's a shame. This poor child would have been better off if she had died. With what lies ahead for her, I'm sure she will wish she would have died."

A shudder of horror swept over the unsuspecting, weary nurse, as Kat ripped the latex gloves off her hands and exited the fatigued examination room.

Chapter 5

Logan slipped quietly into the darkened doctor's lounge and tiptoed over to his wife who was fast asleep. Kissing her on the cheek, he whispered in her ear, "Wake up, dear. You've got to go to work."

Laying on the small cot, Kat rubbed the sleep from her eyes as she stretched and asked, "What time is it?"

"It's eight-thirty and time for the shift change. Stephanie said you've been out for about two hours."

"Whew! I didn't expect to drop off so deeply."

"It finally caught up with you, dear. Hey, you forgot something," Logan stated.

"What?"

"Well! We went all the way over to his house to get it and you left it at home." Logan smiled as he held up the nativity scene now packed in a box.

"Oh, Logan, I did forget. I was so intent on getting here in this weather that I didn't even think about it. But thanks to you, I don't look like a fool and an old man will be very happy, at least for a while," she said.

"And what do you mean by that?"

Reaching down by her side, Kat picked up several folders she had placed on the floor before falling asleep. Opening the top one, she handed it to her husband and said, "Read it. They're the blood tests I just got back on Mr. Trudeau, the man who requested this nativity."

Knowing she wouldn't be handing him the report unless there was something wrong, he pushed it back and said, "Bad, huh."

"Yeah, I'd say there's a distinct probability this man has cancer. I'll have to run a bone scan and biopsy to be sure, but his blood tests show he has a high level of alkaline phosphatase."

"Let's hope it's not as bad as you suspect."

"Just the same, I'll have David Cross look at all of the results, too."

"You know best, but right now it's time to get moving."

"Oh, you're right. You know, I went down to his room as soon as I got the results this morning, but he was asleep, so I came back here and nodded off myself. I guess that should be my first stop," she decided, climbing off the cot and straightening her clothing and hair.

"Okay, then I'll just go back to my office. Catch you for lunch at about one?"

"Oh, don't go yet. I'd like you to meet Mr. Trudeau. Just come up with me to his room. Maybe you'll recognize him," she hoped, pulling him by the arm out of the ER doctor's lounge and up to room 1225.

The door to Mr. Trudeau's room was open and the hospital personnel had just delivered breakfast to the fragile-looking old man. As Kat and Logan entered the room, he was about to take his first bite of food, when he looked up and saw them enter.

"Good morning, Doctor. Did you bring someone else to take a poke at me today? I'm pretty sore from what you did to me yesterday."

Again, a sense of familiarity fell over Katarina like a gentle rain from heaven as she looked into the face of the affable, elderly man. Smiling a broad smile, she said, "No one's going to poke at you today, Mr. Trudeau. I just brought my husband in to meet you. Noel Trudeau, this is Logan Stone. He's the administrator of this hotel at which you are registered."

Reaching to grasp Logan's already outstretched hand, Noel smiled and said, "It's nice to meet you, sir. Your lovely wife, excuse me, I should say the lovely doctor here, spoke of you yesterday."

"As she did of you to me last night. I only trust she said nice things about me."

"Of course, Mr. Stone, only the nicest. She thinks rather highly of you, I'd say," Noel replied with a wary smile and a wink of his eye in the direction of Katarina.

"That's good. I see my training has paid off and today you can't be too sure of that."

"We'll see how well-trained I am later, Mr. Stone," Kat playfully added.

"I think that's my clue to get back to work. It sure was nice to meet you, Mr. Trudeau. I hope your stay here in our hospital is a short one."

"I'm sure it will be, Mr. Stone. When you get my age, you expect a few things to break down every now and then. I'm sure that's all it is. Besides, if we didn't, it would put your wife out of business."

"And me as well," Logan chuckled as he exited the room, waving goodbye and leaving Kat alone in the room with Noel. Pulling out the package containing the nativity from behind her back where she had been hiding it since she came into the room, Kat smiled and said, "I have something for you. I found it last night. At least this is the only one I saw. I hope it is what you wanted."

Noel's eyes lit up like a child's on Christmas morn when he saw the top of his beloved nativity sticking out of the box held in front of the good doctor.

Sparkling with newfound exuberance, he sang, "Oh, thank you, Dr. Stone. Thank you, thank you, thank you. It's already a better day than yesterday. You know, if I've got to be here at this time of year, at least I can be happy. Right?"

"That's right, Mr. Trudeau. Now, how was your night?"

"Oh, please, Doctor. Mr. Trudeau is much too formal. Call me Noel. It sounds better."

"Okay, Noel, but I still need to know how your night was," she gave in.

"It was good, considering," he revealed.

"Considering what?"

"Considering the pain and what I went through yesterday. But the nurses were wonderful. They kept me pretty doped up most of the time so I could sleep."

"Do you still have a lot of pain this morning?"

"It's not as bad, but it's still there. But then, it has been there for so long, I can't remember when I didn't have the pain," he enlightened.

"In your chest?" she assumed.

"No. Not in my chest. I haven't had any pain in my chest. That is, until yesterday. But even that has mostly subsided. It's the pain in my back. I've had a deep, dull, throbbing pain at the base of my spine for months now. Like I said, I can't remember when it started."

"Have you seen a doctor about the pain?" she asked.

"Heavens no, Dr. Stone. It's like I told your husband. When you get my age, you expect to have a few aches and pains."

"Maybe so, Noel, but can you describe the pain to me?"

"I could, but I would rather talk about you."

"I'm not here to talk about me, Mr. Trudeau," she stated a little abruptly.

"There you go again with that Mr. Trudeau. It's Noel," he scolded.

Exasperated by this kindly old man, she tried to explain, "Noel! I don't think that pain in your back is from the basic aches and pains of old age. I believe it stems from something worse." Appearing completely disinterested, Noel sat on the edge of the hospital bed and arranged his prized nativity on the night table. As he was about to place the celebrated Christ child in the carved manger, he abruptly turned, faced Kat, and announced, "Don't worry about me, Dr. Stone. I will be taken care of."

"Wait a minute. I get paid to worry. I think we need to run a series of tests and we need to get them done as quickly as possible," she stated, growing more serious.

Seeing the frown on her face, but seemingly not hearing her words, Noel explained further, "You see this Christ child?"

Nodding her head, she looked more closely at the figure he was holding in his hands in front of her and mumbled, "Yes."

"With Him, I have nothing to worry about, because He has promised to take care of each of us. So, regardless of where the pain stems from, everything is in His power."

Spinning a bit off-balance from his comment, she fumbled, "I appreciate your personal faith, Noel, but that's plain foolishness."

A bit offended, Noel exclaimed, "It's not foolish, Dr. Stone. Christ gives and takes life. And there really is nothing that can be done, if it is my time."

"Oh, but you're wrong, Mr. Trudeau. There are many things that can be done. So, if you will please stop this foolishness, I'll get on with my work."

Refusing to let the doctor treat him like a child, he reprimanded her, "Oh, it is you that is foolish, Dr. Stone. You think you have power because you can treat disease. But your only power is what He has given you."

"Mr. Trudeau, I am not going to get drawn into a silly discussion over religion with you . . ."

"I can see it is hard for you to talk about things you don't understand. You have probably never had an experience with the power that is His," he said, cutting her off.

Not wanting this to go any further, she charged, "What I have had, Mr. Trudeau, is experience with life and death. Every day I help people continue to live. I won't allow someone to die because he won't listen to, or follow the advice of, his doctor." Holding out her hands, she continued, "These hands can prolong life and repair the human body whenever it is injured or becomes diseased. And your body has become diseased. That's why I'm here, out of my responsibility as your doctor and for no other reason."

"Okay, Doctor, you tell me. What lies in store for me?" he succumbed.

"Your blood reports came back signifying something is wrong. Listening to you explain about your back pain convinces me even more. I need to order a bone scan and maybe a biopsy to be sure, but I think it's possible you have cancer," she said, pausing to let her revelation sink in. But Noel just stared blindly at her with a grin on his face.

"Do you understand what I'm saying, Noel?"

Dropping the grin and responding with clarity, Noel declared, "I understand perfectly, Dr. Stone. I understand you really don't know much about what gives life or what takes it away and that scares you. You assume your gifted hands can control life, but they can't. You may be able to repair this body, but you forget the most important part, man's spirit. I know you think I am a silly old man who has no family and doesn't care whether he lives or dies, but I completely understand what faces me. Much more so than you do, Dr. Stone. I have lived a good life and turned my spirit over to Christ. If He wants to call me home, He can do so without any argument from me. However, if it is His will that I should continue to live, then I will do so with a joyous heart."

"But what you don't see is, you have a say in whether or not you are called home, as you put it. With the right treatment, we can sustain life and extend it, but if left untreated the disease wins and you lose. Leaving the complete decision up to something which may or may not exist is stupid. It is like that man I read about who got caught in a snow drift. Frightened, he waited for his God to save him. Twenty-nine days later he starved to death, when he could have walked out to safety on a dry road, less than a mile from where his car was stuck. Noel, I won't let you starve to death, not when a road is so close," she declared with utmost logic.

"Very well, Dr. Stone. You do what you have to do and I won't object. But remember, this God you so lightly refer to is real and has power way beyond what you have. You may control this body with your accomplished hands, but He controls my spirit as well. I know because I have witnessed it many times, in many ways more powerful than you know."

"I'm sure you have," she condescended, getting up to leave.

Unable to let her sarcasm be the last word, Noel stated, "Wait a minute, Dr. Stone, and listen while I tell you a short story."

Stopped in the middle of her exit and a little irritated, she asked, "How long will it take? I don't have much time."

"It won't take very long. Doctor, when I was a young man and before I was married, I volunteered to do some service work with an organization similar to your

Peace Corps. The difference was, we talked of Christ and His gospel, while helping people in their respective communities. During that time, I was assigned to Belgium and I watched people's lives change as they accepted Christ and His principles. One particular example of His power in action comes to mind.

"We had been working with a very poor family, named Defoe. It was a rather large family consisting of a mother, father, and six children ages twelve, ten, nine, seven, five, and two. Mr. Defoe was partially disabled from a deteriorating disk in his back, but his only skills were that of a laborer. In fact, the only work he could find was on a hog farm in a small community west of Brussels.

"We knew the family well and had spent several days helping out on the hog farm. I must say it was very difficult work. Even today, I believe they were some of the hardest days of work I have ever experienced.

"When the Christmas season rolled around that year, we discovered the Defoes had nothing with which to provide a Christmas for their family, and their pride kept them from asking for help. Our hearts were broken because it was the first time in our lives we had ever known someone who couldn't provide Christmas for their children.

"Christmas had always been a joyous time for me. Even during the Great War, mother made sure we worshiped Christ and exchanged gifts. At times throughout my life, it was my only repose. "Broken-hearted as I was, I couldn't let this problem go unresolved. So, I suggested to my associate that perhaps we could help by gathering gifts for the children and playing Pere Noel on Christmas.

"It so happened that at that time, we had just volunteered to work at a social bureau which reconditioned used items so they could be given away to the needy. It was all part of the community's charity. We worked long hours refurbishing everything we could. As we did, we watched for items we could give to the Defoe family. It was hard keeping our little secret, but we managed to wriggle the necessary information about sizes and desires out of each member of the family without being discovered. It took most of December before we met our goal. We knew we couldn't just show up with gifts so we decided to talk to the parents.

"When we shared with Mr. and Mrs. Defoe what we had done for the family, my heart almost burst as tears of joy fell from their eyes. What seemed like such a simple thing to us, to them was magnificent.

"Mrs. Defoe was so grateful, she insisted on imparting of their substance with us. She pressured us into coming to dinner on Christmas Eve. We accepted reluctantly, because we knew they had very little for themselves, let alone enough for us, but it seemed like the right thing to do. Dr. Stone, I remember that Christmas Eve like it was only yesterday. We carefully packed our old Citroen with the gifts we had gathered and wrapped in preparation for our trip.

"The snow had been falling for two days in our little hamlet and at least ten inches had accumulated on the ground. In those days, we didn't have big snow removal trucks, so the snow just piled up. That evening, we set out on what was usually a one-hour trip, praying we would be able to make it up the hill to the Defoe home.

"On our way out of the city, we stopped at a Christmas tree lot, picked up a discounted tree, tied it to the top of our car, and continued on our way.

"The old Citroen slid back and forth mile after mile, but never gave up. It was like we were destined to arrive. After an hour and twenty minutes, the familiar farm fencing and the ornate gateway came into view. Situated at the top of a hill overlooking the valley farm was a large home where the owner lived. About three hundred yards to the left was a small shack where the Defoes stayed, as part of Mr. Defoe's compensation.

"With a carol on my lips, I turned into the driveway. The old Citroen swished back and forth, hitting the deep ruts worn in the old dirt road all the way up to the house. As we slid into the dooryard of their home, we saw their small children peering out the frosted windowpanes. When we opened the door to our car, they jumped up and down with excitement. We untied the tree from atop the car and carried it into the house, leaving the presents safe, secure, and secret, inside our old automobile.

"The children climbed all over us as soon as we walked into the house. When the jostling settled down, we set up the tree and decorated it with a few sparse, well-worn, glass ornaments."

As Noel related the episode about decorating the tree, Kat's mind fell back to the night before when she and Logan stood and studied the sparsely decorated tree in Noel's humble little home. She wanted to say something, but thought better of it and let him continue with his narrative.

"When the tree was finished, Mrs. Defoe called us all to the dinner table. Quickly the children scampered into their assigned chairs with a buzz of anticipation and we settled down in our reserved seats.

"Since our arrival, the children hadn't stopped talking about the feast Mama had prepared for them. They wanted to show us the delicacies, but Mrs. Defoe kept shooing us out of her kitchen every time we tried to sneak a peek. However, the smells of the house let us know we were in for a treat.

"One by one, Mrs. Defoe placed four bowls filled with meager portions of food on the table. When she was finished, her oldest son, Sean, cried out, 'Don't

47

forget the bread, Mama.' Laughing at herself because of her faux paux, Mrs. Defoe diligently went back into the kitchen and brought out a basket filled with small, freshly baked rolls. The sweet aroma of bread filled the tiny house as if it were a giant bakery.

"I looked at the food displayed on the table in front of me and wondered when she was going to bring the rest. I always ate well, but what I saw Mrs. Defoe place on the table wasn't even enough to feed myself and my companion, let alone eight more mouths.

"This, Dr. Stone, is where I learned to trust in Christ. I had read about how He fed the five thousand with just five loaves of bread and two fishes, but I always thought it was a fairy tale. As I sat at that humble table, I said to myself a silent prayer to God asking Him to fill us with the small portions."

Pausing, as if telling the story somehow weakened him, Noel stared straight into Kat's dark brown eyes and said, "Dr. Stone, I have never eaten more food in my life! We ate and ate and ate. And each time we placed the bowl back on the table, there was more food remaining than when we picked it up. I thought perhaps it was just me, but my associate insisted on clearing the table after we had gorged ourselves. Together, we put away the leftovers, marveling that we had to use extra bowls in order to hold all that was left.

"He had heard my prayer, Dr. Stone, and not only did He hear it, He answered it. With a power far greater than I can explain, He multiplied the food set before me, just as He had done when He fed the five thousand.

"Dr. Stone, your power is good and I will submit to it, but don't ever think it is all the power that is available to us. It is not, this I know."

Finishing his account, he turned back to the small night table in his hospital room and placed the Christ child in its appropriate place. While tears streamed down his old, wrinkled cheeks, Kat stood speechless and tried to absorb the transcendental sensitivity which had swept over her.

Chapter 6

Exhaustion was creeping over Dr. Stone as she walked up to the nurses' station and asked, "Sarah, did radiology bring Mr. Trudeau down for his scheduled bone scan?"

"Yes, Doctor. He's been back in his room now for about thirty minutes. I expect you'll receive the report before you go home," Sarah answered.

"I doubt that. Dr. Cross has been called over to St. Francis on a consult and I specifically asked for him to evaluate the results for me. I don't expect he'll be able to get to it until first thing tomorrow morning. Besides, I can't give it enough attention tonight anyway. It's been one of those days, if you know what I mean."

"I do. I seem to have them regularly too." Sarah chuckled and then asked, "Did you look in on the little burned girl?"

"Not yet. I've been saving that for last. Why? Is there something I should know?" Kat asked, knowing that the real reason she hadn't been in to see the girl was that she wanted to postpone viewing the child's misery for as long as possible.

Sensing a little apprehension from the doctor, Sarah calmly added, "Not really. We got her settled in the burn unit and we have a name for the little girl. It's Tiffany Welch. The police say her mother was also burned very badly and is in critical condition over at St. Francis. As of yet, they haven't been able to find any other family members. Right now she's all alone, so I've checked on her about every thirty minutes today. I was thinking she might like to hear another voice. That's all."

"I'll look in on her in just a few minutes, Sarah. By the way, has she regained consciousness yet?"

"No. Not yet. Every once in a while she lets out a little whine or whimper, but she hasn't opened her eyes yet. It's terrible. I'm just glad I wasn't here when they brought her in. I don't know if I could have taken it. I just hate to see little ones suffer."

"I know what you mean, but we have to do what needs to be done," Kat said, putting on a tough exterior for the benefit of the compassionate nurse.

Expecting the cold response from her superior, Sarah asked, "Dr. Stone, what is your opinion about euthanasia? Do you think it's all right to help someone die? I mean, when I look in on that little girl and I see how much pain she is in and knowing it's never going to end for her, I wonder if it might be better if we helped her end it all now?" Sarah's question ended in a soft whisper.

Fumbling for a response, Kat stuttered, "That's a tough question. There is a real rift between doctors on this subject. Some feel it is our job to eliminate the pain and suffering, and others feel that under no circumstances should we intervene. I think it's a debate that will never have a complete answer. But to me, it's a giant paradox when compared to the Hippocratic oath every doctor has taken."

"I guess you're right, but people are going to act on their own moral standards, whether they are right or wrong."

"That they do, Sarah. That they do."

Checking the clock on the wall, Kat excused herself and walked towards the ICU Burn Unit located next to the ER at the large hospital. Pausing outside the private glass cubicle, she gathered her fortitude and entered the compact room. Moving next to the bed, she watched the petite, huddled frame lying on the sterile hospital bed. Systematically, the mechanical respirator forced oxygen into the tiny lungs and moved her wee chest up and down. Her small body was positioned to protect the blistered skin and provided Kat with a panoramic view of the disfigured little girl. The severity of her burns and the seriousness of her condition overwhelmed her.

For a moment, she hoped there was a higher power, someone omnipotent that was in complete control, who would step in and take over. As she pondered the possibility, a small moan slipped out of Tiffany's mouth. Her attention drawn to the sound, Kat watched as the maimed little body receded back into a fetal position of security. A wave of emotion rolled over Kat like a flooding river overflowing its banks and dredged up unwanted memories of the past. Upset, she quietly raged, "Why would a God let something like this happen? Why would He let an innocent child suffer so?"

Caught in a controlled frenzy, her thoughts were interrupted again as Tiffany whimpered, cried, and clutched the IV tubing like it was her favorite blanket.

Meanwhile, Logan had come down from his office looking for his wife. He had moved unnoticed over to the ICU cubicle where he stopped to observe her with the little girl. At the edge of the child's bed, she carefully picked up the bright pink hand of the suffering girl and gently squeezed the fingers together. Unable to read the words forming on her lips, he craned his neck to see if there was anyone else in the small room to whom she could have been talking. Seeing no one confused him, and watching the tears fall from Kat's eyes added to his bewilderment.

Although the fragile little girl couldn't hear the words being spoken, Kat continued talking, "Oh, little one. If I could do more, I would. But I just can't. As powerful as doctors are, there are some things we just can't do. But I promise you, the pain you feel now will eventually stop. I will make it stop. I know there are those who say I could end it all for you, but that is not right and so you must hang in there until it gets better. I will do everything I can to make it easier for you," she sobbed. Leaning heavily on the bed's guard rail, she dropped her head down and rested it on her arms. The tiny, burnt fingers of Tiffany Welch latched onto the larger hand of Dr. Stone and tightened around her first two fingers. Quickly raising her head, Kat looked down into the swollen, distorted face. There was no mistaking the dependent expression behind the grotesque open eyes as she tried to mouth the silent but coherent word, "Mommy!"

Chapter 7

The silent confines of her own car did little to dispel the residue of the emotional purging Kat had just experienced. Her private conflict continued to rage inside her mind like the funnel of a tornado. She wanted desperately to discuss her feelings with someone who would understand, but she didn't know how to bring them up with her husband. So, she silently sat and listened to the soothing music playing on the car's stereo.

Following in the car behind her, Logan wanted to know all about what he had witnessed earlier. He struggled, however, not knowing how to broach the issue. The water was muddied for him by the fact that he wasn't sure he had seen what he thought he had seen. Had there really been tears falling as Kat worried over a patient? Her puffy red eyes when she got into her car seemed to testify there had been, but why? He couldn't remember the last time she had shown any emotion, let alone cry, in a public place.

Finding no answers, he rubbed the bristle of his five o'clock shadow and reflected silently to himself. After a few moments, he thought out loud, "I've got to be careful because I don't want her to know I was watching through the window at the burn unit. So, I'll wait until she brings it up."

Driving up the ramp into the parking garage of their condominium complex, they parked their cars in their assigned spots. Logan got out before Kat and whipped around to assist her with the expected niceties.

"Isn't it good to be home?" he asked, helping her out of her car and walking up to their front door.

"I guess. Most of the time, I have so much to do, I feel guilty about leaving the hospital, but not today. Tonight all I want to do is soak in a hot tub," she said as a freezing gust of wind lashed against her while she unlocked the door to their house.

Shivering from the same gust of wind, Logan warmed himself by rubbing his hands together briskly and remarked, "Ooh! Sounds inviting and I'd love to join you, but I've got some things I need to do and I don't dare put them off any longer."

"What have you got to do that's so pressing?"

"Well, for one thing, I've got to get my Christmas letter off to Mom and Dad. If I wait any longer, it won't get there till after Christmas and you know how upset Mom got last year when it was late," he frowned, helping her off with her coat and hanging it alongside his in the closet.

"For heaven's sake. We don't want that to happen again. You'd better get it done right away," she laughed in bogus sincerity, as she dropped her briefcase on the table and walked into the bedroom.

Following behind her and a bit unsure of Kat's sarcasm, he added, "Don't make fun. This is serious business. I'm already in trouble because I told Mom we wouldn't be there for Christmas. If I forget the letter, who knows what she'll think. You know Mom."

"Yes, I do and I understand. But don't worry about it. I've got plenty to keep my mind occupied as I soak away my worries." Kat sighed, fell back on the bed, grabbed a pillow, and hugged it tightly.

Sensing Kat was making no attempt to get undressed, he asked, "I thought you were going to soak in the tub?"

"I will, but this feels so good. I think I'll just lay here and relax for a few minutes and wind down."

Kat's pressing desire to shed the weight of her day granted Logan the opportunity for which he had been searching. He asked, "And what made your day so worrisome?"

Seeing her opening, but letting it go by, she hesitantly replied, "I don't know. It wasn't just one thing."

"Oh! One of those days, huh? It seems that things mount up at the least opportune time, doesn't it?"

"You got that right," she agreed, making sure her countenance didn't give away her deeper concern. Not sure she could conceal it much longer, she rolled over on the bed away from the direct gaze of her husband, letting the lofty down comforter swallow her weary body. Soothing her head back into another inviting pillow, a quiet sigh slipped through her lips.

Stepping over to the side of the bed, Logan sat on its edge, reached over, and began massaging her shoulders.

Immediately feeling the strength of his powerful fingers, a comfort flooded over her and she said, "Oh, don't stop! That feels so good."

"So, I am of use," he goaded, feeling her tense a bit under his hands in response to his comment. "Seriously! I really want to help. Is there anything you need to or want to talk about? It's not often we get the chance to have an intimate discussion."

Enjoying the relaxation of the massage, Kat pondered his question in silence, wondering how to reveal her true feelings. Thinking there was going to be no response, Logan was about to get up and change his clothes, when he was halted by her answer.

"Well, maybe there is something, Logan. I had a little dispute with Mr. Trudeau after you left this morning and it has bothered me all day long," she sighed, her muscles tensing under his hands when she recalled the dispute.

Surprised that anyone could fight with a nice, old man like Mr. Trudeau, he asked, "What was it about?"

"He questioned my role as a doctor and tried to tell me that I have no control over whether or not he gets well. He claimed the control belongs to some higher supreme power and referred to the source of this power as the Christ Child. At first I thought he might be one of those fanatics who refuses treatment because of religious reasons. So, I was mentally preparing for a fight about his faith being able to heal him, when he told me a story about something that happened to him as a young man. Logan, it really touched me. I have never before heard anyone speak from the heart like that, and I could tell it wasn't a zeal born of naive ignorance, like so many others, but a faith rooted in fact and experience."

Not wanting to embarrass her, but finding it relatively easy to understand, he quipped, "What's so strange about that, Kat? It's obvious he's a religious man. Why else would he have you retrieve a nativity set from his house?"

"I know that. That's not what's so hard to understand. What's hard to understand is how and why it affected me. That's where it becomes difficult. Logan, I know we haven't discussed this very much, but do you really believe in God?" Thinking the question came from left field, he answered, "I don't know. I guess I do, but . . ."

As he was about to offer further explanation, she interrupted him and said, "I know it's a strange question to ask. After all, we have been married for five years and it's never come up in conversation. I've never felt any reason before to believe in God, but something is happening to me and I don't know what it is."

He reflected for a moment, gaining confidence about the issue as he nestled closer to her warm body. "When I grew up, I never went to church or anything like that. There were times when Mom wanted to take me, but Dad wouldn't hear of it. He didn't want any son of his to be a mamby-pamby alter boy."

"That sounds like your father," Kat interjected, as a vision of the crusty old man filled her mind.

"But I had this friend, Ted, in the neighborhood. In fact, he was my best friend when I was about nine or ten. He and his family were always going to church. They were Lutheran, I believe? Anyway, one summer his mom asked my mom if I could go with Ted to Saturday School. Now, I didn't have any idea what Saturday School was, but at nine years old, I wanted to go anywhere Ted went. So, when Mom said it would be okay, I couldn't wait to go. To this day, I can still remember what we learned. They taught us about Shadrach, Meshach, and Abednego in the fiery furnace and how their faith saved them. Now that was very impressive to a nine-year old, but as soon as it was over we had so many other things to do, I didn't think about it again. And I haven't been to church since. But isn't it funny how I still remember all the details about that day after so many years?"

"I don't know, maybe, but then again, maybe not. Maybe that's what I'm talking about. It could be, something touched you that day like something did me today and that's why you remember it. Right now, I can't imagine I'll ever forget how I felt when Noel explained his relationship with Christ, and how he came to know Him. I've never had an experience like it ever before. No one ever took me to church or talked of religious things after Mama died. I was left all alone and it was like no one cared. I very seldom got anything at all for Christmas. I stopped believing in Santa Claus the year after Mama died. I can't even remember when I learned Christmas was in recognition of Christ's birth. I think it was in a world history class I took in high school."

Logan had only known Kat as a distinctly scientific person and so the direction of the conversation perplexed him. Wondering what she was feeling deep inside, he asked, "Kat, do you feel some higher power is trying to talk with you?"

"No! Nothing that dramatic, but it seems like all of my emotions are crashing down on me and that I don't have any control."

"Kat, you need some rest. I don't know what's happening inside you, but I do know you have been working too hard. You're a great doctor, but there isn't another doctor on staff who puts in as many hours as you do. I was worried when you decided to try and keep your practice as a surgeon after they placed you in charge of the ER, and I think my fears are being proven. Things are beginning to catch up with you," he explained.

She considered his logic and hoped he was right. Maybe everything would clear up if she could get some well-deserved rest. Still in deep thought, she sat up on the bed and slid to her feet, then walked into their large closet. Deciding against the comfort of the heated Jacuzzi, she changed quickly into her nightgown and walked back into the bedroom, turned down the comforter, and slipped underneath it.

Snuggling in, she said, "Logan, you go write your Christmas letter to Mom and Dad, and I'll give some thought to taking a vacation."

At her bedside, Logan looked lovingly into her eyes, kissed her on the forehead, and said, "I think you need to get some sleep. I'll whip up something to eat and bring it to you and then I'll write my letter. I love you!"

"I love you, too. And, Logan, thanks for listening and not judging me. I needed that tonight."

"No problem, dear," he replied, giving her a big hug and then walking off towards the kitchen.

After she ate, she lay in bed, where she felt fatigue consuming her, but she couldn't sleep. The events of the day replayed over and over in her mind, each time becoming more poignant. She tossed and turned underneath the safe comforter. Unable to relax, she got out of bed, put on her heavy terrycloth robe, and went into the living room. She walked to the large picture window overlooking the development, parted the curtains, and looked out. Struck by the beauty of the snow-covered neighborhood, she tried to remember the words of a specific Christmas carol, but couldn't. As she looked down the street, she saw a large, lighted nativity at the corner entrance into the condominium complex. Doing a double take, she couldn't remember having seen the nativity before, but tonight there was no escaping it. There seemed to be a special bright glow hovering over the sacred scene. As she stared at it, the words to "Silent Night" finally filtered through her mind.

Chapter 8

Dr. David Cross sat behind a dark, cherry wood desk too big for his cramped office. His short, rotund body was squeezed into a tuck and roll leather chair, while dark eyes peered out through bushy eyebrows speckled with gray. He was studying the contents of the manila folder he had clutched within his puffy white hands. Unable to see clearly, he tried to clear his chronically congested head and placed the folder he was looking at on the cluttered desk in front of him. A pair of bifocal eyeglasses was located and he draped them on a pair of oversized ears. Picking up the folder once again, he squinted at its contents.

Kat knocked on his closed door, but didn't wait for a response before barging in. Looking up from the folder, Dr. Cross grinned while he grumbled, "Come on in and make yourself at home, Dr. Stone."

"Thanks, David. I will," she responded with a sly smile of her own and then added, "Actually, I'm worried about a patient and couldn't wait for your report to arrive, so I came up to get it myself."

"That's not like you, Kat. I've never known you to be overly worried about a patient. In fact, people tell me you don't care about anything but results," he chuckled, his wry smile again spreading over his round face.

Unlike the other doctors in the hospital, David Cross liked Katarina Stone. Birds of a feather, as they say. When he first went into Oncology, he felt like an island unto himself. Unlike the other doctors who tried to balance their lives, his every minute was consumed with medicine. For twenty years he devoted himself to the study of Oncology and was recognized as one of the nation's elite physicians in the diagnoses and treatment of cancer.

Kat was his kindred spirit and right after meeting her for the first time, he identified an appreciation of medicine like unto his own, and that created an immediate, special bond between them.

"David, enough wasting time. Have you had a chance to look at the report of Noel Trudeau's bone scan?"

"Yes, I have. In fact, I was reviewing the scan and the radiologist's report when you came in. I was going to ask you to come up and discuss it, but I guess you read my mind," he answered with a certain melancholy.

"Your tone betrays you, David. How bad is it?" she queried, concern consuming her demeanor.

"It's not good, Kat. There are multiple bone lesions throughout his entire body and they have metastasized in numerous locations, centralizing in his spine."

"Will we be able to contain it and send it into remission?"

"I can't say. It's been left untreated so long, there's really not much we can do. If we have any chance at all, we've got to start treatment right away," David stated.

Grappling with an unexpected surge of emotion, Kat fought to retain her composure as she asked, "What treatment do you suggest?"

"Well, there are several ways we can go. We could use radiation or chemotherapy, but there's a hormonal treatment we could try as well. In my opinion, if he can withstand the approach, I'd recommend chemotherapy, followed by a series of radiation treatments," he advised, watching Kat battle with something bothering her deep inside. When she didn't respond, he asked, "Are you okay with that, Kat?"

Sheepishly answering, ashamed to have been caught in this difficult dilemma, she conveyed, "Sure, David. I just feel so bad for this old man."

David looked intently at a disconcerted Katarina Stone and remarked, "That's not the Dr. Stone I've come to know. I have always admired your ability to

separate yourself from these difficult emotional circumstances."

"Well, I hate to disappoint you, David, but I guess
I am human after all."

"Nice cover, Kat. But seriously, what's bothering
you?" he pressed.

"I don't know, David. For some reason this old
man has gotten under my skin, causing emotions
I've never felt before. Frankly, I'm beginning to
worry," she revealed, hoping David might shed
some light on why she felt the way she did.

Looking at the fear reflected in her eyes, he comforted her by saying, "My good doctor, there's nothing to worry about. You're just experiencing what
happens to the rest of us all of the time."

"What are you talking about?"

"Well, Kat, most of your patients get transferred
from the ER physicians to specialists in other
departments. Even as a surgeon, most of the time
you are called in on a consult, but the rest of us
are with our patients from the beginning of treatment to the very end. It's not easy separating your
emotions when you watch their personal suffering
every day."

"Well, what can I do about it?"

"Kat, you talk like it is some sort of treatable disease. It's not. It is perfectly natural. My only advice
to you is to be patient and weather the storm."

"So, what you are saying is, I'm not losing my mind after all."

"Very astute, Doctor, but the reality is, it's just the opposite. I think you're actually finding something inside you never knew you had and that's quite normal. Now, would you like me to come and explain things to your patient?"

"No, David. Just help me with the treatments. I can handle the patient part. Besides, this is something I need to work through myself. But thanks anyway."

"Okay, Kat. Just let me know when we can get started. Remember, the sooner the better," he cautioned.

"I'll remember. In fact, I'll go down right now and talk to him. If we can schedule something for tomorrow, I'll let you know," she said as she exited through the door and left Dr. Cross rubbing his double chin.

Kat was true to her promise to Dr. Cross and went straight from his office down to Noel's room. Opening the door, she found him, eyes closed, reclining back in his bed with the radio tuned to a station playing Christmas carols. The familiar strains of "I'll be Home for Christmas" streamed from the speaker clamped to the pillow right by his ear. At first she thought he was asleep. Then she saw his lips move, as he silently sang along with each word of the chorus to the well-known song. Clearing her throat, she got his attention. He sat up in bed and smiled his warm, ingratiating smile at his visitor.

"Welcome, Dr. Stone. I've been waiting for you. You're later than usual," he observed, looking over at the small clock on the table behind his nativity.

Staring straight into his dark brown eyes, she wondered if she really was that predictable. Checking her watch, however, she saw that she was running about an hour later than she wanted to be.

"I did that to keep you on your toes, Mr. Trudeau."

Bristling, Noel scolded, "There you go again with that formal Mr. Trudeau. I thought we had an agreement. It's Noel."

"We did, Noel, but I forgot. I apologize, but I don't normally call my patients by their first names," she explained as she reached down and grabbed his chart from the holder at the end of the bed.

"I'll bet you've never had a patient like me before," he laughed.

"You're right about that, Noel. You're one of a kind." She smiled back.

"I'm glad you finally noticed, Doctor."

Looking over the night's report in her hand, she asked, "Have any problems last night, Noel?"

Noel pushed himself up and rested on his side and said, "No. Not last night. Things went pretty well. I must have been pretty tired, because after they gave me my pain pill, I dropped off to sleep and stayed that way all night."

"That's good, Noel," Kat tried to comfort, feeling uncomfortable with the small talk. Looking up from the chart, she saw him staring right at her, so she marched forward with her news. "Noel, the reason I was late this morning is because I was consulting with Dr. David Cross. He's a specialist in the study of cancer here at the hospital. I asked him to review your bone scan and blood tests to confirm my suspicions."

As she was about to continue, he interjected, "And from the look on your face, Dr. Stone, I'm sure he did."

"He did, Noel. There is no doubt about it. You have cancer and it's pretty extensive. It probably originated in your prostate and has moved throughout your body. The largest lesions are in your spine, explaining the severe pain you've been having there."

Letting her news settle in for a few seconds, she watched as Noel absorbed the words she had spoken. Thinking he would say something but getting no response, she continued, "Since it has gone undetected for so long, I can't give a very good prognosis. We need to begin treatment as soon as possible, if we hope to have any success at all. I have asked Dr. Cross to conduct the treatment. He suggested a regimen of chemotherapy followed by radiation treatments, and he would like to start tomorrow."

His eyes never left the doctor as she delivered the terrible news and he could see how difficult it was for her. So, finally breaking his personal silence, he said, "Don't look so somber, Dr. Stone. I know you will do your very best to get me well and if we need to start tomorrow, we will. But remember, I am not alone and my peace will not be shattered. I know Christ will comfort me through my ordeal."

Kat sensed a unique sincerity in his humble words and added, "I'm glad you feel that way, Noel, because chances are you will get very sick from the chemotherapy. Each patient reacts differently, but most get quite ill from the treatments. You will lose a lot of weight and most of your hair. You see, chemotherapy kills the cancer cells, which are growing out of control. But in the process good cells die as well, which can make you very sick. I promise we will monitor your reaction to the treatments and will make sure it is not more than you can handle."

"I am also confident that Christ knows my limits and won't permit me to suffer any more than I can handle," Noel replied, revealing to Kat yet another measure of the old man's inner strength. Growing tired of the morbid subject, he changed the topic. "Let's not worry about me, Dr. Stone. I hear you are taking care of a badly burned little girl."

Showing a little bit of frustration from Noel's indifference, Kat stated sternly, "Don't change the subject now, Noel. I need you to understand how serious this is. Your chances aren't really good and we need to do everything we can, because your life hangs in the balance."

"Then do everything you can, Dr. Stone. But don't try to change me. I've spent too many years on this old earth to change now. What happens will happen and I trust you to do what's best. But you'd be better off helping that little girl get better," he smiled, with a smile that melted the ice of her stern demeanor.

"Noel, you're impossible," she said, but as she said it, it hit her: how does he know about Tiffany? Moving around to the head of his bed, she looked down into his eyes and asked, "And just how do you know which patients I am treating?"

Laughing just a bit, he revealed, "It's not hard, Doctor. I ask about you. The nurses who look in on me are very helpful. They have taken me on a tour of this entire floor. Yesterday, I overheard a couple of them talking about you, so I asked them what it was that was bothering you. They explained you were upset about a little girl with severe burns who you treated the night before. I asked them to take me to see her and they did. I sat outside her window and watched her for a long time."

It upset her that she was the topic of discussion between her own patient and the nurses, and it caused her to lose sight of what she was trying to find out, so she asked, "Who told you that, Mr. Trudeau?"

Not breaking his smile, he just continued, "Who told me is not nearly as important as the fact that I know. And by your reaction, I can tell they were right. I understand you thought it would have been better for this little girl to die, rather than live with her burns. Is that right?"

Flushed from embarrassment, Kat turned away and moved over to the window, angry at the judgment of others. Seeing that she didn't want to talk about it, Noel tried to soften the situation by consoling, "It's all right, Dr. Stone. It's a normal response. We all think it is best for things to end when we don't understand why things happen and what lies in the future."

Turning around to face him, she couldn't control her temper any longer and she erupted, "This time you are wrong, Noel. I know what lies in the future for her. A life of misery. A grotesquely deformed face, without a nose or any ears. People staring at her all of the time and wondering why she is such a monstrosity. While other children her age play together, she'll be left the outcast, only to have others laugh and poke fun at the freak." Pausing briefly to catch her breath, she was completely carried away with passion as she drove on with her rampage, "The physical pain will never subside as she suffers through all those skin grafts. Fresh, new, pink skin trying to heal itself, when underneath is only an open wound, as the plastic surgeons have a hey-day using her as a guinea pig. They'll try every new trick of their trade trying to make her look a little bit more normal. And if that isn't enough, there are the emotional scars from having suffered in a fire like that. There will be nights she'll wake up screaming thinking it is happening all over again, only to find out it's just a dream, but no one will be able to comfort her. Psychologists will play with her mind, trying to make her ordinary inside. Contrary to what you say about Christ and how He has power, He didn't stop the fire that burned little Tiffany and now she has to suffer. Yes, Mr. Trudeau, Tiffany Welch would have been much better off had she died," she finished fuming.

Waiting for a minute, letting quiet fill the space of Kat's verbal assault, Noel leaned back against his bed. Gathering strength, he looked up and called Dr. Stone closer to his bed, making sure she could hear, then very quietly he said, "Dr. Stone, you have so much rage bottled up inside you, but it's all misplaced. I wasn't judging you or Tiffany. I was just making an observation."

Further embarrassed from her inability to control her undulating emotions, she stuttered to apologize but Noel cut her off. "You are very schooled in medical training and what you say about little Tiffany could very well be true, if all we had were man's learning and understanding. But we don't. We have knowledge from on high. Yes, Dr. Stone. I know Christ has power and He could have stopped the fire, but He didn't. Nor did He stop His own ridicule and agony, though He could have. Instead He suffered. When people spit on Him and cursed Him, He turned the other cheek just like He taught. In the depths of His deepest despair, when all of the pain and anguish of the world's suffering fell upon His shoulders, He didn't stop it. Even as He hung on the cross being illegally crucified by His enemies, He asked His father to forgive them. What you don't realize, Dr. Stone, is that Christ suffered for all of us. Not just me and a few who believe in Him, but everyone. You, me, and Tiffany. Right now He knows more about the pain she is in than even you do. But He also knows there is more in store for her than either you or I realize."

Feeling a burning inside she didn't recognize, she pulled up a chair, leaned near the old man and said, "But Noel, if He knows, why does He let her continue to suffer? If He could stop it, why does He let it go on?"

"Ah, that, Dr. Stone, I do not know. But I do know she is not alone. I know Christ loves little children. Many times He gathered the children around Him, and because of His love for them, He wept. I'm afraid, Dr. Stone, the why cannot be answered. But I know we can't judge what lies in the future for such a lit-

75

tle thing. With His help, she may rise above all the adversity she has to face."

"It's not likely, Noel. The odds are not in her favor. Let's face it, life is cruel. Hatred abounds and with the disfigurement she surely has, her future can't be very bright."

Understanding her position very well, but wanting her to understand his more fully, he leaned forward and softly said, "Dr. Stone, maybe this will help. There will be people who will love and adore little Tiffany no matter how she looks. Christ taught that we are to look beyond the outward beauty of a person and instead look for the inner beauty. He wants us to find the beauty of the spirit and I know many people will."

"But Noel, that's just hope. And I'm glad you're so positive. But I don't agree."

"Doctor, when you picked up my nativity, did you happen to see the pictures on the mantel of my fireplace?"

"Yes, I saw several. One specifically of you, and I assumed your wife," she answered, suddenly feeling nosy.

"Remember the picture with a young family at the Grand Canyon?"

Nodding, Kat felt the warm, hospitable surroundings of Noel's charming home descend upon her as she remembered.

"Well, that was my daughter and her family."

"But I thought you didn't have any family."

"I don't. They all passed away before me and are now waiting for me to come join them," he explained.

"I'm sorry," Kat said, wishing she had kept her mouth shut.

"That's all right, Dr. Stone. You didn't know. But I think you would like to know about my grand-daughter, Jenny. She was the youngest in the picture and was about six years old when it was taken." He smiled, fond memories obviously filling his bosom, as tears welled up behind his eyes.

"She was very pretty. I remember. She looked just like her mother. You must have been very proud," Kat commented.

"I still am," he smiled broadly. "She was quite pretty. Once! About two years after that picture was taken, they came to Chicago to visit me and their grand-mother, Maria. Her father was very successful and owned his own airplane. So, they just dropped in one day and surprised us. After a wonderful five-day visit, it came time for them to go home and start school. You see, they lived in Texas, where my son-in-law was an insurance bigwig. We went out to Midway Airfield to watch them leave. Maria and I stood and watched as their little plane raced down the runway and took flight. As it climbed into the air, it caught an unusual down draft, throwing it to the ground. It crashed and burst into flames just beyond the end of the runway."

Kat stifled an audible gasp as she stiffened in her chair, but Noel just moved on fighting back the flood of tears ready to overflow. "Everyone was killed instantly, except little Jenny. But by the time anyone could get to the wreckage, she was burned beyond recognition. For a long time no one thought she would make it. My wife, Maria, and I prayed more fervently than we had ever prayed in our lives, but we didn't pray for Him to help her. We prayed for her to die. We didn't want her to go through all of the things you enumerated earlier. We loved her too much. She had no parents, no brother or sister, only an old grandma and grandpa who couldn't take care of her. The doctors warned us that she wouldn't live very long because her lungs had been severely damaged. Besides, Maria's health had been failing and we just weren't equipped to raise a little girl who was going to need so much care. We prayed and prayed, but our prayers weren't answered . . . we supposed . . . because Jenny didn't die, she lived. After months in the hospital, with doctors from all over the country using her as a guinea pig just like you said, we finally got to take her home. Maria and I were scared to death. We were sure we weren't going to be able to handle it. Dr. Stone, my faith has never been tested as much as it was tested then. Many a night I laid awake and cried to my Lord asking for help."

Curious beyond normal curiosity, Kat sat on the edge of her chair and pleaded, "And did He help, Noel?"

"In ways I never expected, Dr. Stone. It wasn't easy by any means and Jenny did face all of the things we worried about. But an old man and woman learned more about love than we had ever known.

"Our lives changed drastically, as you can well imagine. At first, Jenny's condition demanded our complete attention and Maria waited on her hand and foot. Then the doctor told us it was time for her to start doing things on her own and that she needed to go out in public. Well, we tried and we tried, but she just wouldn't progress. Then Maria came up with an idea. Christmas was approaching and Jenny loved Santa Claus. Although she hadn't been out of the house for more than two years except to see doctors, we decided Christmas was our chance. But Jenny said no. She kept telling us she was too ugly and people would be afraid to look at her. We tried to make things easier, but it just didn't work. Then one day Maria was reading the newspaper and read that Santa Claus was going to be at the five and dime store just a few blocks away from our house. So we laid a plan to take Jenny out to see Santa.

"Even though Jenny was almost ten at the time, emotionally she had regressed and was more like a six- or seven-year old. At first she wouldn't even think of it, but Maria convinced her that Santa wouldn't think she was ugly. He would think she was beautiful, because that's how Santa was. He loved all the little children. So, Jenny finally agreed to go.

"We worried and worried as the day approached and when the day arrived, we prepared with anticipation to go see Santa. Maria had knitted a little woolen cap for Jenny to wear, because her hair never did grow back right and as yet she wouldn't wear a wig. So, Maria dressed her and placed the new little cap on her head.

"We all got into the car and drove the ten or so blocks to the store in silence. We could feel Jenny's fear, as if large, strong hands were gripping our shoulders. In the parking lot at the store, we shed a few tears before we summoned enough courage to go inside. Maria took one of Jenny's hands and I took the other as we escorted her into the store.

"It was a Saturday and the little store was packed. I watched as people craned their necks to get a better look at the poor, disfigured girl as we walked down the aisles trying to find Father Christmas. I wanted to go over to each of them and give them a shake, but I didn't dare leave Jenny's side. As we got to where Santa was stationed, our worst fears were realized. In front of us was a line of children waiting to sit on his knee. Reluctantly, we took our places at the back of the line and tried with all of our might to shield little Jenny from the gawks and comments of the other little children. You know, sometimes little kids in their innocence can be so cruel, as they were that day.

"We didn't know it, but shopping in the store that day, looking for something to buy for his girlfriend, was a young college student. He had seen us when we first came into the store and as we went to get in line for Santa, he quietly left the store. But he returned, and when he did, we were about to place our Jenny on Santa's knee. As we did, he pushed his way to the head of the line, amidst the cries and jeers of the other children. Our little Jenny sat there on Santa's knee frightened almost to tears, when this young man stepped up and knelt in front of her, pushing a bouquet of roses into her lap. No matter how long I live, I will never forget what he said."

Unable to continue because his tears were flowing like rain in a thunderstorm, he wiped his eyes and tried with great difficulty to clear his throat and stop his sobs.

Leaning over to comfort him, tears streamed down her own face, but she summoned enough control and said, "It's all right, Noel. It's all right."

Shortly, Noel gained a measure of composure, grabbed Dr. Stone's hand, and squeezed tightly. While in an emotional whisper, he repeated, "I'll never forget, Dr. Stone . . . this young man kneeling in front of my little granddaughter with all of her grotesque scars and her bright pink skin, saying, 'These are for the most beautiful girl I have ever seen.'"

Again he cried uncontrollably, heaving with deep sobs. Holding onto his hand and weeping as well, Kat waited for this moment to pass. After several minutes of sobbing in silence, Noel looked into her wet eyes and concluded, "Dr. Stone, from then on Jenny wasn't a burden to us anymore. In fact, until she died six years later, she brought more joy and excitement to an old man and his wife than they deserved."

Chapter 9

The corner office on the fifth floor of the University Hospital was one of only eight executive offices in the building with windows to the outside world, and this one belonged to Logan Stone. For the last twenty minutes he had been watching snow flurries, forgetting the paperwork on his desk and then Katarina bounced in with unexpected enthusiasm.

"Pack it up, dear. I've got a surprise for you," she announced.

"Surprise? You, Dr. Stone, have a surprise for me?" he asked incredulously.

"Yes, I do. I called this afternoon and made dinner reservations for seven-thirty at Lowery's. I knew you could use a good piece of red meat."

"Ah! The unhealthiness of it all, but seven-thirty? What are we going to do until then?"

"I was thinking about how you've been going on and on and on about me needing to get rid of this place and relax a bit, and then it occurred to me how long it has been since I have walked the city streets and enjoyed the decorated storefronts. So, I thought we could do some window shopping."

"Sounds great. Let me grab my coat and we'll be on our way," he exclaimed. They left his office and headed for the car.

Logan wanted to park in an underground garage, but Kat's enthusiastic persuasion won over and he parked just off Michigan Avenue. Holding on tightly to his arm like a young couple in love, they sauntered down the avenue watching the shoppers bustle back and forth with their packages.

About a block after they started, Kat pulled up short and shrieked, "Oh, Logan! Let's go in there."

"Where?" he asked.

"In the popcorn store."

"It'll spoil your dinner," he teased.

"That's okay. This used to be the best. I used to escape here when I was younger."

Giving in, they walked into the warm store and were surrounded by the fragrance of freshly popped popcorn. Standing at the counter like a kid in a candy store, Kat looked at every flavor available. Making her choice, Logan decided on the same and ordered two small bags of cashew and caramel.

With popcorn in hand, they exited the cramped store as Logan remarked, "I'll have to say, if this tastes half as good as it smells, we're in for a treat."

Already chomping down on her popcorn, Kat could only nod in delightful agreement. They walked in silence except for the occasional crunch of popcorn and stopped and looked at every exquisite trimming in the beautiful store window displays.

After a while, Logan checked his watch and commented, "We'd better get moving if we're going to make our reservation."

"Okay, but there's still one more store I want to visit."

"And what store's that?" he asked.

"I'll show you," she said as she grabbed him by the arm and escorted him into a quaint little toy store.

Inside the door, Logan looked at the wide array of specialty toys, but his eyes came to rest on his wife's eyes, full of unsuspecting innocence. Smiling to himself, happy with the manifested change in his otherwise stern wife, he lovingly asked, "What do you have to buy here?"

"I just wanted to pick up a little toy for Tiffany."

"Who's Tiffany?"

Looking at him like he had just overlooked the most obvious of facts, she enlightened, "She's the little burned girl I have been telling you about. After what I experienced today, I just had to stop and get a little something for her."

"What happened today?" he asked.

Her spirits buoyed from the evening's events, she looked him straight in the eye and said, "Oh, Logan. I learned about beauty. Not the beauty of the body, but the beauty of the spirit. I learned that people will love and cherish little Tiffany, even though she will be scarred and deformed."

"And how did you learn that, Kat?"

"Noel told me about his granddaughter who was severely burned in a plane crash, and how that experience taught more about how to love and what to look for, than anything he had ever experienced. He told me how people they didn't even know showed love and compassion to her, and how their fears about her future were all dispelled. It touched me so much that this afternoon I took Noel down to meet Tiffany. Logan, here is a man who is dying, and yet he won't let anyone feel sorry for him. He told me to stop worrying about him and to focus on getting Tiffany well. Today I watched him play with a little girl who most people wouldn't even want to look at. Even though she can only lay there in her bed, they played and played. He made her laugh and, for a brief moment, forget her pain and suffering. He stayed with her until she fell asleep. I could tell it was hard on him, but he wouldn't let on, not one little bit."

Logan watched what seemed like a metamorphosis in his wife and was amazed at how deep it seemed to be, causing him to conclude, "Noel must be a very special man to have effected such a change in you."

"He is, Logan. In fact, I've never met anyone like him before . . ."

Smiling inwardly to himself, pleased with Kat's youthful exuberance, he didn't hear the rest of her explanation.

Chapter 10

"Good morning, Stephanie. How was last night?" Kat asked as she swung into the ER.

Surprised by the unusual upbeat mood of the doctor, Stephanie responded, "Same ol', same ol'! We were busy. We had a gunshot victim, an auto accident, and an elderly woman with a coronary, just to mention a few."

The faint pulses of "We Wish You a Merry Christmas" played in the background. Kat suggested, "Maybe we could turn that up just a bit? I'm sure anyone trying to listen is having a difficult time hearing the music. And if we're trying to lift their spirits, it'll be hard if they can't even hear it."

"Sure, Dr. Stone. Is there anything else you need me to do before the shift change? If not, I'd like to go home. It's very slow and I'm scheduled back in six hours on a switch with Dana. So, if you say it's all right, I'll slip out about thirty minutes early."

"I don't have anything specific for you. I'm going to check through the reports from yesterday and last night, then I'll go up and do rounds and check on some patients. I have Mr. Trudeau's chemo scheduled for today and I need to be there to check his reaction. When you are finished, leave a note for Sarah about where I'll be," Kat instructed as she walked back into the small cubbyhole she called an office.

She sat in the cramped quarters while she quickly reviewed the files of the patients treated in the ER over the past two days. Normally, she hated detail work like this to pile up, but she had enjoyed yesterday so much, she didn't feel guilty about having to catch up today. Getting back to her typical diligence, she pored over the details and signed each report. It was now time to do her rounds, but she checked first to make sure the shift change had occurred without incident. She found Dr. Anderson treating a young boy with a fracture of the radius bone and Dr. Smoot examining a pregnant woman having false labor. Convinced everything was in satisfactory condition, she climbed the back stairs to the second floor with the hum of the carol "Joy to the World" on her lips.

Dr. David Cross was standing behind the nurses' station on two as Kat emerged from the stairwell, and she hurried over to speak to him.

"Good morning, David!" she smiled, confirming her cheeriness.

"It's almost afternoon, Kat," he answered blandly.

Checking her watch and thinking David must be wrong, she said, "So it is. I've been backlogged with reports downstairs and I wanted to catch up on them this morning before I came up. Is everything ready for Mr. Trudeau's treatment today?"

"That's why I'm here. I wanted to come down a little early and talk to the patient about what to expect and help him feel comfortable. You caught me checking his chart before I went in. I needed to make sure he hasn't had any food in the last twelve hours," David explained, holding up a chart marked Noel Trudeau for her to see.

"When I went home last night, he was ready to get started today. He is confident we will do our best. You won't have any problems with him."

"Sounds like the perfect patient, but it's not him I'm worried about. It's the chemicals. They work wonders, but not without a price, if you know what I mean. Would you care to introduce me to this patient of yours?"

Looking squarely into his eyes, she smiled and ignored his indifference as she walked with him in the direction of Noel's room.

Lucille Grant, a lanky, red-haired nurse, stepped from behind the nurses' station and ran to catch them as she called out, "Excuse me, Dr. Stone. Addie just called from your husband's office. There's a special meeting underway in his office and she said for you to drop whatever you're doing and get up there right away. It sounded like it was extremely important."

Kat caught the earnest disposition of the generally happy-go-lucky nurse, turned and offered her apologies to Dr. Cross, and left. Striding away quickly, she went over in her mind every remote possibility about what this meeting could be regarding. Unable to come to any conclusion, she exited the elevator and stepped briskly into Logan's outer office. Seeing Addie immediately, she said, "What's going on, Addie?"

Addie shrugged her shoulders signaling she didn't know, but moved over to Logan's door, knocked briefly, then escorted Kat inside.

Upon entering his inner office, Kat immediately felt the weight of the air which hung over the threesome already in discussion, huddled around the table next to Logan's desk. Without delay, Logan stood, as did the other gentleman in the room, acknowledging Kat's entrance. "Dr. Stone," Logan said, "This is Andrew Phillips from the State Welfare Department, and this is Helen Henshaw, a social worker from his office."

Kat frowned at her husband's formality as she shook hands with the two visitors and then took her seat. Upon hearing the words 'welfare department' and 'social worker,' she immediately put up a shield of distrust between herself and the visitors.

Giving her a quick glance, Logan explained, "I've asked Dr. Stone to participate in this meeting because she has been treating the patient in question, and I felt she could give us the greatest insight on how or what would be the best way to proceed. So, Mr. Phillips, if you wouldn't mind, will you please start over from the beginning? I think it would be helpful."

Andrew Phillips nodded his head in agreement and started again. "As I stated before you arrived, Dr. Stone, Sandra Wilkinson, a patient over at St. Francis, died yesterday. The police and federal agencies have been trying to find any surviving family members of Ms. Wilkinson.

"What they found was that Sandra Wilkinson was orphaned when she was three years old and raised in a series of foster homes throughout the state of Illinois. Although she had no immediate family during the time she spent in the foster homes, Sandra gave birth to a daughter about six years ago. She gave the child a last name different than her own, making it difficult to track her down. We found that she is a patient here at your hospital. Her name is Tiffany Welch."

Shock rocketed through Kat's mind like a bolt of lightning, staggering her internally. As she tried to capture control and cope with the revelation, the room seemed to spin as Mr. Phillips continued his explanation.

"Tiffany's birth certificate shows the father as unknown. It's not uncommon. A lot of girls in her situation do the same thing. Either they don't know who the father is, or they don't want the father to know there is a child. So many of them who get into trouble think they can raise the child by themselves, but they forget to leave any information in case there's an emergency."

Seeing the utter devastation in Kat's face, Logan intervened and said, "What Mr. Phillips and Ms. Henshaw are concerned with is finding a foster family that is equipped to provide the extended care Tiffany is going to need when she is released from the hospital. They wanted your estimate of what would be needed and they were hoping you could give them an approximate date when Tiffany might be discharged."

Kat was about to answer when Mr. Phillips jumped in with further information, "Actually, that's only part of the reason, Dr. Stone. With Tiffany now a ward of the state, her care is our responsibility. Our research shows that Sandra Wilkinson had no health insurance on herself or her child, thus forcing Medicaid or State Welfare to assume the costs of her medical care. Unfortunately, University Hospital is not one of our approved providers. Therefore, we are going to have to transfer Tiffany over to St. Francis, where she can be treated by one of the providers on our list."

Out of breath like someone had hit her in the stomach, Kat stumbled for the appropriate words as her temper flared. "What? What are you saying? That Tiffany isn't getting the proper treatment here?"

Andrew Phillips tried to shed more light on what was obviously misunderstood, as he said, "No. That's not it at all, Dr. Stone. It's just that the State Welfare Department is not equipped to pay for the medical bills accumulated here at University Hospital."

"It doesn't seem too difficult to me. Our billing structure is not any different from that of St. Francis. We'll simply bill you and you can pay us," Kat suggested.

"It's not that simple. Payments come from government agencies and with the budget cuts and all, if you're not an approved provider, they won't pay."

"Oh, I see. It's government red tape double talk. If you don't have an answer, fall back on budget cuts and an inability to pay bills," Kat seethed, fury building behind her cold steel eyes.

Logan could feel the powder keg beginning to rumble, so he interceded, trying to diffuse the volatile situation. "This is such a new hospital, we haven't been placed on some insurance company lists yet and that includes welfare funding from the state. That being the case, the treatment being given to Tiffany can't be reimbursed."

Cutting him off like she would an impudent child, Kat exploded, "So this is about money. Is that it? Money? Let me enlighten everyone a little bit. We have a young girl, who three days ago could have died. Our entire staff did everything we could to save her, knowing all the time that she was going to be deformed and disfigured. But that's okay, because that's what we do. We save people. But, now that we've saved her, this poor little girl faces a life full of turmoil. If her disfigurement was not enough, now she's lost her mother, the only family she has ever known. Then to top it all off, you want to take her away from the only stable thing she has had since she was burned. I'm sorry. I just can't fathom this. She knows us here and she looks forward to the nurses who visit her every day. She cries out for me to come and comfort her whenever she's alone and you want to destroy all of this because of a little money?"

Helen Henshaw tried to offer a bit of explanation to Kat, having been stung by her accusations. "That's not it at all, Dr. Stone. You don't see the whole picture. To you, this is just another patient who you will take care of and then, when she is well, you will send her on her way and never think about her ever again. We can't do that. We have to put together a plan that will work for her for the rest of her life—a plan that we can live with every day—and the only way we can do that is to work within the established system."

"Ms. Henshaw, I see the whole picture better than you think I do. I know how Tiffany will be shuffled from one foster home to the next. She will be given to families who have taken in more children than they can handle so they can get a few extra dollars every month. None of them will be equipped to handle her or be able to help her when she needs help the most. All you can do for Tiffany is make her another statistic. It seems to me, Mr. Phillips explained her mother was nothing more than a product of the failure of your system, and now you want to put her daughter right back into the same system."

"I don't know where you get your information, but the picture you paint is not accurate. Now, I didn't say the system was perfect. Sometimes it works and sometimes it doesn't, but one thing we do know is, without it nothing works," Ms. Henshaw argued.

"Well you're right about one thing, Ms. Henshaw. This time it won't work, because I won't stand for it," Kat erupted.

Logan observed, "It's not your decision. From what I see, there's nothing we can do. We must abide by the state's wishes."

"He's right, Dr. Stone. If need be, we'll get a court order forcing you to turn her over to St. Francis," Mr. Phillips declared.

Livid with anger and unable to control it any longer, Kat stood and yelled, "Then I suggest you try and get one, Mr. Phillips, because I won't give in. I will fight you every step of the way. I'll keep this tied up in the courts until my treatment of Tiffany is finished. Besides, who in the legal system is going take a little homeless girl out of my care and this hospital for the sake of a stupid system, simply because the care is free? If I were an attorney, it would be called pro bono. I assure you, all of the care of Miss Tiffany Welch will be absolutely free, gratis, until she is released from my care."

Startled by her outburst and the content of her threat, Logan sought to calm his wife as he said, "You know we can't do that, Dr. Stone."

She spun on her heel and faced her husband, balanced on the brink of losing total control, and commanded in a voice that no one could mistake, "Logan, I don't care what you have to do, but I expect you to make the necessary arrangements for Tiffany Welch to remain here at University. And until I have complete confidence that this has been accomplished, this conversation is over."

As she stormed out of the office, the door crashed behind her and left the remaining trio completely speechless.

Chapter 11

Sitting in the chair she had dragged into Tiffany's room with her, Kat just watched the bandaged little body. Breathing on her own now, the room was peculiarly quiet without the rhythmic beating of the mechanical respirator. Savoring the silence, she reviewed again the events which had devoured her, ever since they happened two days ago. She thought her temper would have pacified with time, but she was wrong. It had grown with each passing hour as she calculated the futility of the situation. Try as she might, she couldn't put the smug pretenses of Andrew Phillips and Helen Henshaw out of her mind. They were like all of the others she had known in the system. On the surface they wanted you to feel their compassion, but when push came to shove they were more concerned about their system than the children.

Her anger had spilled over into her personal life. The only words she had spoken to her husband in the last two days were mandates reiterating her threat to him. Regardless of her emphatic injunction, he rejoined with ineffectual efforts and lost hope, causing the strain between the two of them to mount with each passing hour.

Startled when Tiffany's groan broke the peaceful silence absorbing her, she smiled with pride as the little girl clutched the bear dressed like a doctor that Kat had given to her.

When she had presented it to her, Tiffany had quickly named it Doctor Kat and hadn't put it down since. Even in her sleep she clutched it tightly, seeking whatever security it could provide. The unrestrained ebb of emotion quickly changed to anger as Kat felt the depth of her helplessness. Even if Logan could arrange for Tiffany to stay, Tiffany ultimately lost, because at some time in the future she would have to be turned over to a system that didn't always work.

Refusing to accept the inevitable, Kat hadn't been able to bring herself to tell Tiffany about her mother. Her mounting distress gave aid to her fear that the information might slip out from one of the nurses, so she came in early to wait for Tiffany to awaken.

Again the bandaged child moved and rolled over onto her side. For a moment her eyes darted open and then closed again. Reaching up and seizing the wrapped hand, Kat whispered in her ear, trying to wake her. Fighting hard to stay amid the peace and comfort of slumber, Tiffany battled to remain asleep. However, when she recognized Kat's smiling face nestled next to hers, she forced the drowsiness away.

"Dr. Kat," she rasped, her throat dry from breathing through her mouth.

Kat picked up a sponge affixed to a stick, like a lollipop, sitting in a cup of ice water and wet her patient's parched lips. Picking up the glass, she bent a straw so Tiffany could take a sip of the cool liquid to moisten her throat as she said, "Good morning, sleepy head."

"Good morning, Dr. Kat!"

"How do you feel this morning, Tiff?" Kat asked, an affection in her tone she had been hiding from everyone else.

"Okay, but it hurts."

"I know, sweetie, but that's because the medication from the night is wearing off. I'll give you some more in a minute, but first I want to talk to you. Okay?" she asked, hoping the little girl wouldn't suspect anything unusual.

"Sure, Dr. Kat. I like it when you come to visit. It's like having my mommy come," the swollen little face beamed.

Heartache throbbed inside Kat's chest, pounding like a sledgehammer laying rail. Gently cupping Tiff's swollen face with her hand, she whispered, "That's what I want to talk to you about. Your mommy."

Immediately she bubbled with enthusiasm at the thought of her mother and cried, "Is she going to be able to come and see me today? Nurse Sarah said she got hurt in the fire too and that's why she hasn't been able to come and see me. She will, though. As soon as she's better she's going to come. Right, Dr. Kat?"

Choking back the tears and wanting to rip away from Tiffany's tender grasp, Kat wondered if she could pull this off. With all her courage in tow, she squeezed the tiny hand and said, "I'm sorry, honey, but your mommy isn't going to come. You see, she was hurt very badly in the fire just like you were. Only she isn't going to get better."

Drowning in a sea of emotions, Kat barely heard Tiffany's tearful plea for an explanation. "What do you mean, Dr. Kat? Why isn't Mommy going to get better?"

Thoughts swirling all through her head, Kat felt a tear drop onto her hand from her eyes. Using her free arm, she reached into the pocket of her lab coat and pulled out a handkerchief. Wanting to flee from the room, her emotions tightened their stranglehold as she heard Tiffany ask, "What's wrong, Dr. Kat? Does Mommy have to stay in the hospital forever?"

Knowing she couldn't escape, she tried to smile through her tears at the small child as she said, "Tiff, your mommy can't come and see you, because she went to heaven the other day."

Not understanding what Dr. Kat was trying to explain to her, she asked, "Is heaven a nice place, Dr. Kat?"

"Oh, yes, sweetheart. It's a very nice place," she whimpered, imprisoning the deeper sob straining to get out.

"Is it close to Chicago, Dr. Kat?" she asked, hope rising inside her.

"No, darling. It's not close to Chicago."

"But, if it's a nice place, won't Mommy come and take me there to be with her?" Tiffany cried.

Kat sunk deeper into the whirlpool of her emotions, not knowing what to say as she choked on her tears and concluded, "Yes, Tiff. Maybe someday your mommy will come and get you, but not for a long time."

"You mean, not until I'm better and can go home from the hospital, don't you, Dr. Kat?"

Hating herself for saying it, but knowing it had to be said, Kat added, "Longer than that, I'm afraid, Tiff."

She wanted to say more, but was cut off by Tiffany's sobs and her next question, "If it's longer than that, Dr. Kat, who will take care of me when I go home?"

Losing her grip on her feelings, Kat dropped her head and gently rested it on Tiffany's breast, completely overcome as she wept, "I don't know, sweetheart. I don't know."

Chapter 12

Rolling to his side, Noel retched in the small plastic tub for the umpteenth time. Finishing his ordeal, at least for the time being, he laid back and propped his head against his pillow, completely expended of all energy. As he floated in and out of consciousness, he remembered Drs. Cross's and Stone's warning. They told him about what to expect, but even their best efforts couldn't describe the experience he was living. About every hour his body convulsed, trying to rid itself of some unseen organism. Racked with pain and nausea, Noel struggled to stay awake. He gazed directly at his sacred nativity and sought support and comfort from it as a recess from his ordeal. He smiled when the music and words to "O Holy Night" played on his little speaker, brightening his spirits for just a moment or two.

Pushing the door open, Kat absently entered Noel's room. With strength enough to only roll his head, Noel acknowledged her presence. Seeing her puffy red eyes and the streaks in her makeup, he hoarsely inquired, "What's the matter, Dr. Stone?"

Not hearing the raspy whisper from the feeble old man, she seemed to ignore his petition and picked up his arm while she checked his pulse.

About to have a blood pressure cuff strapped on, Noel pushed with all of his strength. Finally getting her attention, he drug his arm out of her hands as he said, "I don't know what's bothering you, but it's obviously something very deep. It's written all over your face."

Looking down at the weakened man, she sighed, "Oh, Noel, it's terrible. Little Tiffany's mother died and I just told her about it this morning."

"That is terrible," he coughed.

"What makes it worse is that she doesn't have any family to fall back on. No one to love and comfort her. The vultures from state welfare have already been here."

"Don't lose hope, Dr. Stone. We never know what's in the future," he said, trying to buoy her up.

"But Noel, I do know. I grew up in foster homes. My mother died when I was six years old and my father abandoned me shortly thereafter. I was bounced from foster home to foster home and nobody ever cared. I've seen children added to a home already packed because the welfare department didn't have the next family approved yet. Some were more concerned with their monthly stipend than the happiness of their wards. Noel, some of them were actually vicious people who didn't think twice about slapping us around."

"Dr. Stone, that isn't always the case. We have to have faith."

"Noel, when you have seen what I've seen it's hard to have faith. Especially when it comes to Tiffany. She's going to be a freak. It's hard enough for a normal child, but with someone like Tiffany, foster parents just can't give enough attention to someone with her special needs. The kids are like dogs fighting over a bone trying to get a little attention from the parents. I'm telling you, Noel, it's hopeless. And the state can't wait to get their hands on her. They already want to transfer her over to St. Francis."

"Why do they want to do that? Don't they know she is receiving the best treatment she can get right here?"

"It's money, Noel. It's purely money."

"Well, you're not going to let them take her, are you?"

"Not right away, but it's only a matter of time before the courts intervene and order me to turn her over to them," she relinquished, giving up hope.

"Don't lose faith, my dear. You never know how things are going to turn out," he wheezed.

"I know. You've already said that, but it's hard. Noel, how do you do it? How can you be so cheerful all the time? You never seem to lose hope, even in the midst of despair."

Gathering his thoughts and strength at the same time, he picked his words carefully and said, "It's really quite easy. I love life and I love people. Dr. Stone, if Christ gave us anything, He gave us the gift of love. If we carry it with us all the time, it has the power to change our lives."

"Whenever I ask you any question, you always answer with an oration about Christ. Does everything about you revolve around Christ?" she asked for understanding.

Laying his head back against his pillow, he weighed his comments. He wanted to make sure she could discern them as he said, "That's a difficult question to answer, Dr. Stone. I would like to say yes, because I want Him to be the focal point of my life. But sometimes I'm weak and I let other things interfere. I can say that I try to make my life revolve around Him, but it's not easy."

"Well, you do that better than anyone I have ever known," she observed.

"That's very kind of you, Dr. Stone, but all I do is try to keep Christmas in my heart every day."

"Wait a minute. What do pine trees and opening presents have do to with this?"

"Dr. Stone, it's not just opening presents and decorating trees. Christmas is a symbol which represents everything Christ taught us. You see, He was born so long ago, it's easy for us to place Him on the shelf with all of our other decorations when it is over. What I try to do is keep Christmas in my heart every day."

"But why is Christmas so important to you, Noel? What does it really mean?"

Noel closed his eyes for a moment to organize his thoughts. When he opened them, he seemed to draw strength from a higher power. Raising the head of his bed into a sitting position, he said, "The greatest event that has ever happened in the history of the world was the birth of Jesus Christ. That alone should cause us to treasure the experience of Christmas for life, but we don't. We get caught up in everyday living, burdened down with bills and trying to find pleasure. The reality is, happiness is found in His birth, life, death, and resurrection. Picture it, Dr. Stone. Bright light beaming down from the heavens across the diverse Bethlehem countryside, when concourses of angels gathered to announce His birth, shouting hosannas and crying, *Glory to God in the highest, and on earth peace, good will toward men.*"

His voice trailed off into a whisper and he had to wait for a few moments to gather his strength, but then he continued, "The magnitude of this event is found in those hosannas. Although there has not always been peace on earth since His birth and man has not always shown good will toward each other, the events and the annunciations of that night have inspired man throughout the centuries. Even during the dark depths of war, when one man was pitted against another in hate, the influence of Jesus Christ's birth and the message He brought changed lives for the better, forever."

Once again Kat felt herself being drawn to the old man's narrative. However, she saw how difficult it was for him to speak so she placed her hand on his shoulder, letting him know it was okay to wait before he continued. While they waited, she asked, "I've heard how it changed your life, but what about others? Maybe it changed your life because you wanted it to change it. You know, the power of the mind is an awesome thing."

"History is filled with many examples of how Christ and His message have altered countless numbers of lives. Let me try to tell you about one," Noel began very softly.

"The memory of my early life was filled with war's reckless torments, as it crashed into what was an otherwise lighthearted young man's existence. I was born in the coastal community of Marseille, France, to Jean and Edythe Trudeau. I was the oldest of three children, but I was the only boy. My sisters, Vera and Cheri, were three and four years younger respectively. We were the perfect family. Papa was a hard-working father and Mama was a doting mother.

"The beautiful sea and countryside of my homeland was a sanctuary to this young boy who spent his time romping through the grass and the flowers of his environment, chasing any stray dog or other animal I could find. That is, until the war came. I'm talking about what is now known as the Second World War, but to us it was simply The War," he coughed. Kat quickly got him a cup of water and held the straw to his lips. He weakly sucked through the straw to ease the irritation in his throat.

When he had had enough, he continued slowly, "My innocent days of hope were dashed when my country, like many others, plunged into the heart of the conflict. Papa's pleasant manner soon disappeared, being replaced by a furrow in his brow that grew deeper and deeper, as his shoulders began to slouch from worry.

"For a boy of thirteen it was awfully confusing. The details discussed by Papa and his associates were mysteries to me. Oh, I knew my geography and I could place the names of the various countries I heard Papa and Mama talk about, but I didn't know the importance of what they discussed.

"Papa had joined a group of other men from Marseille. We now know it as the OSS and they met every night laying plans, as Papa called it. I wanted to know those plans, but Papa never would tell me. My life was ahead of me and my dreams included everything. Little did I know that just a few years into that future, I would wonder if there was any hope left at all."

Again, he stopped, breathing heavily from the exhaustion. Finally he continued, "You see, NAZI Germany had just taken control of my native land and their tentacles permeated into our little hamlet.

"Our community of Marseille was nestled right on the sea, but it branched up into the lush, dark green terrain of farmland. Most of the homes were spread throughout the countryside, but there were several concentrations of homes around the one industry boasted of by Marseille, Compagnie de Gernale Nationale. It was this industry which made us such a prize for the NAZI government. Right after they took control, they focused their attention on our little plant, converting it to produce war articles. In no time at all, munitions were being pumped out on a daily basis and armed sentries, dressed in black uniforms with the death's head medallion fastened about their necks, were stationed all around the small plant to protect it from any outside intruder."

Kat watched as a fear, based on experiences from long ago, swept across Noel's face as he spoke, "Fear gripped our little community and Papa and Mama cautioned me all the time to stay away from the plant. But to a thirteen-year old, it contained too much intrigue, especially since I had to pass it every day on my way to and from school. So, instead of racing home every day, I'd stop and talk to the sentries. At first they didn't understand a word I spoke, nor did I understand their language. After repeated visits day after day, though, they soon learned a little French and I learned German. I have to say that I was much more successful in learning German than they were at learning French, and in no time at all we were conversing fluently in German. One night, Papa came home extra late from his OSS meeting. We were just about asleep when Papa called us together against Mama's better judgment. We knew instantly it was serious by the tenor of Papa's voice and his overriding of Mama's objections. When we were all sitting down in our little living room, Papa started to update us about the war and tell us what was happening to the Jewish families all over Europe, including the families in our own community.

"Even though we had heard rumors before, it rang truer coming from Papa. When he finished with his explanation, he grew even more somber. Putting his arm around Mama, he spoke in hushed tones as he presented a problem to us. Papa wanted us to take a Jewish family into our home and hide them in our attic. The Greenberg family had already lost a father and a brother. Mother Greenberg and her daughters, Sara, a girl four years my senior and little Jackie, six years my junior, were all that were left. Papa explained to each of us the risk he was asking us to take. He told us that if we were caught, we would suffer the same fate as the Greenbergs, which meant sure death.

"Dr. Stone, fear was knee-deep in our little home that night. Papa said he wouldn't even consider bringing them into our home without the complete agreement of every family member. At first, Mama screamed no in disagreement, her intense desire to protect her own family rising above her charity. But Papa reasoned so well. He talked of Christ and His love and how our lives should be centered in Him, rendering love and service to others. Then he turned to Mama and asked, 'Oh, Mama, what would Christ do?'" Needing to stop because he was so weak, Noel panted like a dog to regain his breath and willed himself to go on.

"There has never been a silence so deafening as the silence which surrounded us after his question. Tears streamed down our faces, while at the same time fear beat louder and louder in our hearts. After a long pause and a brief family prayer, we finally agreed. But we had no idea how acute the pressure would become when the Greenbergs finally moved into our home."

Deeply affected by Noel and his family's courage, Kat said, "I remember when I was growing up, I read

The Diary of Anne Frank. It was my favorite book. I took courage from her experiences, which gave me strength to handle my own tribulations. I have great admiration for what they went through, but I never thought I would meet someone who helped families like hers. It must have been very harrowing."

She wasn't sure he had heard her or even if he was awake. His head lay still on the pillow and his eyes were closed. His chest heaved up and down and then he spoke, "It was, Dr. Stone. After the Greenbergs joined us, we became afraid to talk to anyone for fear of revealing our secret. Every night Papa warned us about the danger we were in, until it got to the point that we couldn't bear it any longer. We started picking at each other. It seemed that Cheri and Vera were at each other's throats all the time. Mama and Papa started yelling at us more often and they wouldn't let anyone stop by our house at all. As the war progressed, the NAZIs put more pressure on our little city. We were already living under a curfew, but they raised it an hour, forbidding anyone to be on the street after eight P.M. Then they began rationing our food, keeping as much as they dared for themselves. Papa had seen it coming. So, before we really needed to, we stockpiled all the food we could. Even after the rationing started, we tried to conserve because we didn't know how long the war was going to last. But even with our foresight, it didn't take long for our little family to run short of food, especially with three secret mouths to feed. It reached a critical stage in the winter of 1944. Rations had been deeply cut and we didn't even have enough food for ourselves, let alone the Greenbergs. Tempers flared frequently as our stomachs ached for food.

"Mama tried with all of her courage to make our lives seem normal. Even though we were losing hope quickly, Mama brought out our Christmas decorations and placed them around our humble home when the joyous season arrived. When Papa got home, he was enraged. He yelled at Mama about how the NAZIs forbade any celebration of the Christian holidays. His logic was that if they found out about the decorations, they would find out about the Greenbergs and we would all be killed. Mama listened as patiently as she could and then she let Papa have it. Crying in an uncontrollable rage, she shouted that the NAZIs had taken everything from her. Her family was starving and afraid to speak. They couldn't go out at night and every minute of every day they feared for their very lives. She cried that they might take everything else, but they weren't going to take away her faith in God and her love of Christ. She let him know in no uncertain words that she was bound and determined to celebrate at any risk. Knowing that Mama was just about at the end of her rope, Papa gave in and helped her place selected articles around the house. Mama's most cherished Christmas piece was her olive wood nativity, which she placed on the mantel over the fireplace."

Kat was about to ask the obvious question, when Noel struggled to raise his hand and nod his head, yes. His love of Christmas and his nativity now made perfect sense to her, so she simply remained silent.

"One night, about three days before Christmas, our crisis reached a sober stage. We had had very little food for over six months and Papa had promised Mama he would bring something home that night. But when he got home, he reported that the food line was so long that by the time he got up to the front all of the rations were gone. Turning away from Mama, Papa broke down and cried. Dr. Stone, Papa never cried before. I'm sure the strain upon him was more than he could bear. Mama suggested we needed to make the Greenbergs go elsewhere. She contended that our family came first and since we had arrived at the point that we couldn't take care of our own family, it was time to stop hiding and feeding some- one else. Argue as he might, Papa couldn't get through to Mama anymore, so he called a special family meeting that night. We gathered around our little table in the kitchen. Mama took the nativity off of the mantel and placed it in the middle of the table, praying it would inspire our decision. As he explained our predicament, Papa spoke in a low voice, hoping the Greenbergs upstairs wouldn't hear us.

"As he was speaking, there was a loud rap on our front door. Fear shattered our concentration and gripped all of us like clenched pliers. Spinning quickly to look at the clock on the wall, we noticed it was an hour after curfew. Everyone knew that if a knock came upon your door after curfew it only meant one thing. The Gestapo had discovered you. Fear froze us to our chairs as the loud knock pounded the door once again. Papa looked at each of us as if it were the last time we would see each other, and then the door rumbled with the hammering a third time. Getting up from our little table, his legs almost collapsing underneath him, Papa inched over to the door. Mama moved quickly, trying to hide the tiny nativity on the table, but Papa directed to her to her seat just before he unfastened the lock. The hammer was starting a fourth time when Papa finally opened the door.

"As we huddled together at the little table, Papa stared into the dark, deep, cavernous eyes of a uniformed NAZI official. Not a word was spoken, Dr. Stone. Only one small action. Oberfuhrer Boris Schmidt, with his large six-foot, six-inch frame filling our doorway in his black dress uniform, thrust out his arm, sending chills down our spines and Papa reeling from the doorway in fear. Dangling at the end of his hand was a large, old Wehrmacht-issue cooking pot. Motioning for him to take it, he pushed it closer into Papa's face. Terrified to do anything else,

Papa reached out his awkwardly shaking hand and took hold of the old worn pot. Without saying a word, Oberfuhrer Schmidt dropped his arm to his side, spun on his heels with expert precision, and quickly strode away from our door.

"Stunned, Papa could barely push the door closed and we all gasped for oxygen, letting our lungs release the air we had previously thought could have been our last. Moving over to the table, Papa set the pot down and Mama took off the lid. Inside the pot was porridge—more porridge than our family had seen in two weeks. It was a miracle, Dr. Stone. Our family was starving and the love of Christ interceded. It touched the life of a man who denounced all that Christ taught."

Noel's chest heaved back and forth as the strain of telling his story was taking its toll, but he pushed on, "Do you realize Oberfuhrer Schmidt put his own life in danger by coming to our home that night? He showed us that love was more powerful than hatred, even in the midst of war. In the heart of battle, he extended an olive branch of peace. For one small moment, amid the outcries of hate surrounding our humble family, there was peace on earth and good will was exhibited towards men. Those were the same annunciations that were given by the angels at Christ's birth, but we didn't fully understand the depth of our miracle until later. Although we rejoiced in happiness and thanksgiving that night, it was later I learned of the true love of Oberfuhrer Boris Schmidt." Noel had to stop again because any strength he had was just about used up.

"The war was almost over. The Americans had landed at Normandy and, day by day, they recaptured our land from the Germans. It wasn't long after our city had been given back to us that we all rejoiced in the streets, celebrating like we hadn't been able to celebrate for a long time. The war had consumed six years of our lives. When it started, I was thirteen. Now we could finally see an end to the war. Our hopeless future reigned with glorious promise. We sang and we danced and we partied and then it happened. I was dancing in the middle of our main street, finally at an age where I could join the French troops in battle, when I heard the dreaded sound of a German motorcycle approaching. For five years I had feared that sound. Spinning around, hoping I was mistaken, I saw it coming. It was bearing down straight at me in the middle of the street, its rider shouting out my name. Screeching to a stop right in front of me, Oberfuhrer Boris Schmidt yelled out my name in his fearful German accent. His uniform had been ripped to pieces as he had battled to get back to our little hamlet, once again putting his life in danger. Straddling his bike, he spoke in quiet tones below the din of excitement, making sure I understood the native tongue that he had taught me when I had made my daily visits to him at the plant. He pulled me close so only I could hear him. Fear was pulsating through my veins with every beat of my heart. He said, 'How are the Jews?' Uncertain that I understood him correctly amid the fear streaking throughout my being, apprehension revealed itself in my expression. Once again he asked more pronounced, 'How are the Jews?'

"Shaking inside, I tried to answer, but the words wouldn't come. Finally I whispered, 'You knew?'

"Looking straight into my eyes and boring through me like a laser, he said as a humble smile curved his lips, 'Yah, I knew!' Then with silent tears streaking his face, this monster of a man asked, 'Why do you think I brought the porridge?'"

Bound, as if by chains from his own emotions, Noel stopped while he choked back his own tears. Looking up into Kat's moist eyes, he said, "The true miracle that night was Christ's love, not only for our family, but for the Greenbergs too. He used a NAZI official to deliver it, forever changing the lives of those involved. Dr. Stone, if he can create a miracle under those circumstances, he can create a miracle for little Tiffany," and then he fell back against his bed, totally exhausted.

Chapter 13

It wasn't the first time Kat had left the hospital without telling him. However, it was the first time she had left in the middle of the afternoon with no intention of returning. The past three days had frustrated Logan. At the best of times, Kat could be obstinate and stubborn, but this recent obsession with Tiffany Welch confused him. She acted like she was the only person in the world who knew what Tiffany needed and that just wasn't the case. Driving home, he resolved it was time for her to stop her sulking and he reasoned that tonight was the night.

When he pulled into his parking stall, he saw Kat's Saab already parked. Striding into their home, he called out, "Kat! Kat!" No response sent him into the bedroom, where he changed his clothes and then began again to look for his wife. The door to her private office was closed and he suspected Kat was locked inside. It was her private sanctuary, a place where she could escape whenever life got difficult.

So, facing the closed door, he rapped, then waited until he heard her mumble, "Come in."

The knob turned in his hand as he opened the door and entered.

"You didn't let me know you were leaving. I checked all over the hospital and nobody seemed to know where you had gone," he started.

"You could have paged me. I would have answered the page," she responded curtly.

"That's not the point and you know it, Kat. Ever since our meeting with the people from the state the other day, it's been you against the world. And I don't like it," he stated with added emphasis.

"I can't help it if you don't like it, Logan. There are a lot of things in life we don't like. Tiffany doesn't like the fact that she got burned and she doesn't like that fact that she has to go live with someone she doesn't know. But, like it or not, she has to deal with it. Isn't that what you told me just the other day?"

Spinning around to face his wife squarely, he said, "It's not the same thing."

"But, Logan, don't you see? It is the same thing. At least to poor Tiffany it is."

"But it's . . ." he tried to continue but she cut him off.

"This morning I broke the awful news to her about her mom. I tried to explain that a loving family would be found who would take care of her and treat her like their own, even though I don't believe it. And do you know what her response was?"

"No."

"She cried, Logan. She cried because her mother died. And she cried because she has to do something she doesn't want to do."

"And I'm sure you painted a glowing picture for her," he interjected.

"I did! Despite what you may think, I'm not heartless. I would do anything to make Tiffany feel better."

Feeling the reality of her anguish, he acknowledged, "I know you would Kat, and it must have been very difficult."

"It wasn't easy, I assure you. However, it was a lot easier for me than it was for Tiffany."

"That's only temporary though, Kat."

"You're wrong, Logan. For Tiffany the heartache will never end. Oh yes, she's coping with it now. But it won't even sink in until she leaves the hospital and there's no mother to go home to."

"That's where you're wrong, Kat. She will have a mother to go home to. I'm seeing to that," he justified.

"I mean a real mother. Someone she knows and loves. You can send her to any woman in the world you want to, but she won't be her mother."

"But what else can be done, Kat? You know she can't stay at the hospital forever."

"I know, Logan. I know. That's why I'm having such a hard time with this. I'm trying to come to grips with the fact that no matter what I do, there's no way of changing the situation," she sighed, dropping her head into her hands, almost in tears.

"Kat, Tiffany isn't the only little girl in the world who has lost her mother."

Looking up through tears, she cried, "But she is the only one I care about, Logan. Can't you understand that? I'm sorry, but I fell in love with a little girl I can't help."

"Dear, you have to trust other people. I know your feelings about the system, but give me some credit. I did convince them to let her stay at the hospital until she's ready to go to a home. And that was no small feat. Just have some faith. Things will work out all right."

"Now you sound like Noel. That's what he keeps telling me. All you need, Doctor, is to have a little faith," she mocked.

"He's right, dear. As much as we would like to think otherwise, we can't do everything by ourselves. We have got to rely upon others to do their job."

"So everyone keeps telling me."

"Kat, I know how you hate the system and I know it's because of how the system treated you. That's why I'm asking you to trust me. I'm working with Mr. Phillips and Ms. Henshaw, and I'm going to make sure what happened to you doesn't happen to little Tiffany. I even went down and spent some time with her today."

"When did you do that?" she asked, a bit surprised.

"After you left this afternoon. We needed to talk to her about her situation and we needed to get to know her a little better. I knew you wouldn't allow Ms. Henshaw to do it. So, I volunteered. I must say, she is a special little girl and she really thinks highly of you."

"I'm afraid her trust is misplaced, Logan, because I can't help her."

"You're wrong, Kat! You can help her—in ways you don't even know about yet. But you have got to stop worrying about things out of your control."

"That'll be easy. Everything seems out of my control lately."

"What do you mean by that?" he asked.

"Oh, nothing."

"I know it is something. What is it? Have you done something concerning Tiffany that I don't know about?"

"No! But Tiffany isn't the only patient giving me a hard time right now."

Immediately, Logan knew to whom she was referring and added, "The elderly man on two. Noel something-or-other?"

"Yes. Noel Trudeau."

"What is it? Did you finally determine why you think you know him?"

"No. It's watching him die that bothers me."

"Are you sure he's going to die?"

Thinking about his question, she responded, "I don't know and that bothers me more than anything else."

"I see," he said, like a light had just come on in his mind. "It's not your concern for your patients that's bothering you. It's finding out you're only human that bothers you."

"How dare you say that?" she accused.

"It's easy, Kat. Every day you hold the life of some individual in your hands. And you rely upon the skill of those hands to determine whether or not they live or die. You are so good at your craft that you get a feeling of invincibility. Well, wake up and smell the roses, dear. You're not God. You aren't invincible. And whether you like it or not, life isn't fair. And there is not one thing you can do to change it."

"That's unfair. I . . . I . . . I . . ." she stuttered.

"It might be, Kat, but it's true. It's not Noel's cancer or Tiffany's burns that is bothering you. It's your inability to manipulate the outcome of those situations that you can't stand," he explained, looking straight into her hollow eyes.

Kat just sat behind her knotty pine desk, where she let her head sink into her hands. Logan walked from behind the chair and over to the window and just stared out into the cold, leaving her to ponder in silence. Finally, she broke the agitated tranquility of her office as she said, "I'm sorry, Logan. You're right. My problem is that I'm beginning to realize how human I really am, but it's not easy. It's not easy wanting to change something and knowing I can't. Take Tiffany, for example. I know I can't change her situation, even though I would like to change it. Now, I'm beginning to accept that. But does it hurt? You bet it does. It hurts me more than it should, because I was taught that doctors weren't supposed to hurt."

Walking behind her desk, Logan sat on the edge and placed his arms around his aching wife. Raising her head with a nudge from his arm, he offered, "Maybe doctors aren't supposed to hurt, but friends are. And for a change, Kat, you're more than a doctor. You're a friend."

Kat let her head fall against his arm. Tears rolled down her cheeks as the truth of Logan's statement hit home. Together, they sat there for several moments enveloped by a sweet, calming peace. Eventually, Kat cut in and asked, "What am I going to do?"

"That I don't know, my dear, but you've got to have hope. Looking into the future without hope can be a very discouraging thing."

"Now you sound like Noel again."

"He must be a remarkable old man," Logan teased.

"You're right, again, Logan. He really is a remarkable man. He teaches me something almost every time I visit him."

"Like what?"

"Well, take today for example. He taught me about what he called Christ's greatest gift, the gift of love. He told me a story about when he was growing up in France. His family hid their Jewish neighbors in their attic for most of the Second World War."

"Really?" he exclaimed, nudging her away so he could look into her eyes.

"Yes!"

"That must have taken some courage," he added.

"It did. You see, they were discovered just before the war ended and that's where the love of Christ comes in. Laying his own life and military status on the line, the German official who discovered they were protecting a Jewish family had compassion for them and instead of reporting Noel's family, actually assisted them."

Kat paused to let the full impact of her words settle and then she added, "You can say what you want about Noel Trudeau, but he is definitely a man of undaunted faith."

"And, from what you've said, he thinks you need to have a little of that faith. Am I right?"

"More than just a little. He thinks that is the one area of my life that is deficient. And right now, I think he might be correct," she conceded.

"I don't know if it's faith or if it's hope that you need. I suspect it's hope," Logan tried to explain.

"Noel would say they are one and the same and that Christ aids in providing you with both," she added, waiting again for her words to take effect.

Feeling that needed to be the last word, Logan asked, "Have you eaten?"

"Yes, and there is a T.V. dinner in the oven for you, but it's probably dry by now."

"Great. Tasteless and dry, but that's okay. I'm starved and I've got to eat something. After that, I'm going to bed. It's already late," he said looking at his watch.

Kat wasn't ready to join him, so she said, "Don't wait up for me. I've still got a few things to do."

Taking her at her word, Logan kissed her on the cheek and went into the kitchen where he devoured the tasteless dinner, cleaned up after himself, and went to bed.

⚬✗⚬

Small, almost inaudible sniffles filtered through the cadence of the machines sustaining life throughout the burn unit. Tiffany lay alone on her bed in her cubicle with her head raised just a little bit. The hollowness she felt inside let her know she was really alone. All afternoon she had wrestled with what Dr. Kat had told her. She didn't want to go live with anyone else. She wanted her mom, but Dr. Kat said her mom wasn't coming back and they would find a nice family to take care of her. She didn't want a nice family. She wanted her own family. She told Dr. Kat's husband that earlier, but he had said she really didn't have a choice. "Why? Why don't I have a choice? Why couldn't they just let me stay at the hospital? Dr. Kat and Sarah could take care of me here," she softly pleaded out loud to no one. But even the thought of staying at the hospital couldn't fill the empty pit she felt inside.

Rolling from his side to his back, Logan stirred from a deep sleep. Reaching over to touch his wife, he found her bedside vacant. He sat up and saw the clock flash one-thirty on the digital screen. Deducing she had fallen asleep in her office, he climbed out of bed to go wake her. As he walked down the hall, he could see the light from under her door. Opening the door, he found the office empty. Uncertainty swept over him and he called out, but no one responded. Concerned, he began looking in all the rooms, his anxiety mounting with every step. Then he noticed that the drapes to the large window in the living room were pulled open. Moving to the window, he looked out. Seeing nothing, he scanned up and down the street. Finally his eyes landed on the lighted nativity on the corner and the solitary figure in front of it. Squeezing his eyes tighter, he focused, recognizing his wife kneeling in front of the sacred scene.

Chapter 14

The uncontrollable dry heaving had given way to a new dilemma for Noel. He woke early in the morning coughing and spewing something from his mouth. Running his hand over his face and back through his hair produced an unexpected fistful of white hair. The soft, silver strands seemed to cover his entire bed. With difficulty, he pushed himself up and over to the side of his bed and turned on the light. It took a while, but he shuffled over in front of the mirror where he was met with an awful sight. His once beautiful hair had been replaced by what appeared to be a ratty old rug. Large patches of scalp peered through a scraggly mess of thin, silver hair.

At first he was frightened by what he saw, but then he remembered Dr. Stone's warning. He was going to lose his hair as a part of getting well and so he should be prepared when it happened. But nothing could have prepared him for what he saw reflected in the mirror. Standing in front of the mirror, he pulled handful after handful of hair from his head, and then placed each clump carefully in the drawer of his portable night stand. He pulled and pulled until no more hair came out. Then he carefully cleaned up the bed and floor, placing all of his hair safely in the drawer.

He had barely finished cleaning when breakfast arrived. Even though he knew he wouldn't be able to keep it down, he ate anyway. It was really nothing of substance, just clear liquids he made believe was a hearty meal.

After eating, he laid back on the bed and relaxed, wondering if his hair would grow back. In the middle of that reverie is where Kat found him when she came into his room. Looking him over, she instantly remarked, "I see you've lost your hair, Noel."

Smiling up at her, he winked and replied, "No, Dr. Stone. I haven't lost my hair. It's right here in the drawer." Pulling the drawer open so she could peer inside, some of the lightweight hair floated out.

They both broke into hearty laughter. Kat was so amused, she had to pull up a chair and sit down until she could gain control. Finally she sighed, "That was a good one, Noel. I've never heard that one before."

Smiling at her, he added, "Well, what could I do? I couldn't stop it from coming out, so I decided to keep it. Every last hair." Picking up a few errant strands, he punctuated his point by putting them back in the drawer and closing it tight.

"Noel, you never cease to amaze me. Most people are scared to death when they start to lose their hair during chemo, but not you."

Waving his hand to stop her, he asked, "Do you want to know the truth, Dr. Stone?"

She nodded her head yes.

"I was scared when I first saw it, but then I remembered that you told me it was a by-product of getting better. It was then I knew I couldn't do anything to stop it, so I decided to make the best of it."

"I wish it were that easy for me."

"What do you mean?" he asked.

"Dealing with problems. You seem to know the perfect way of dealing with whatever life tosses at you. On the other hand, I don't seem to be able to deal with any of life's curves at all."

"That's not what I hear," he inserted.

"Ah. Oh. What have you heard?"

"I have it on good authority that you make one little girl here in this hospital feel pretty darn good."

"Where did you hear that?" she asked.

"From the horse's mouth. I went down to see Tiffany last night. She told me you're the best thing that's happened to her since she arrived here."

"She did? That was awfully nice of her, but I really haven't done much."

"Then do more," he chirped.

Shaking her head in disbelief, she said, "That's easy for you to say. But I think you forgot, we're dealing with Katarina Stone here and not with Noel Trudeau."

With a sly, mischievous grin, he smiled, "I know we are, but I've got this feeling. You've got something up your sleeve, and you don't even know about it yet."

She lifted her arms up and mocked him, as she looked down her sleeve and said, "There's nothing in here, Noel."

"That's what you think, but I think better. There's something up that sleeve that's going to make that little girl extremely happy, because it's Christmas."

Kat shook her head, amazed at what she was hearing and was about to get up out of the chair, when an idea hit her. At first, she couldn't believe it. It seemed so obvious. She was shocked she hadn't thought of it before. Then she looked over at Noel who sat on his bed with a big grin from ear to ear, and he exclaimed, "You've got it, haven't you?"

"Yeah, Noel. I've got it. Santa Claus helped your granddaughter cope and he can help Tiffany cope as well. All I've got to do is make sure she gets an audience with Jolly Old St. Nick."

Noel was pleased with the excitement which swept through his doctor. She seemed to sparkle with enthusiasm, something he hadn't seen in her before. All of a sudden though, it seemed to vanish as quickly as it had come, and she exclaimed, "Who am I trying to fool? I don't know anything about making a little girl happy."

Before she could continue, he interrupted her and stated, "But, I do. And if you're nice to me, I'll help."

"Oh, would you, Noel?"

Nodding his head yes and smiling even wider, he promised, "Of course."

Kat pulled the chair closer to the bed and with pencil and paper in hand, they put their heads together to map out what they were going to do.

Chapter 15

The crisp morning air tingled with excitement as Logan and Kat worked their way through the crowded rush hour streets towards the hospital. Taking the appropriate exit off of I-90, Logan asked, "Is everything ready for today?"

Kat bubbled with a childlike giddiness as she answered, "I think so, but I'm nervous. I want everything to be just right."

"Don't worry, everything's going to be just fine. What time are you going to take Tiffany over to the pediatrics ward?"

"Santa is scheduled to arrive at about two. Before that, there will be singing and a few games. I thought I would take her over at about one-thirty or so. I took her gifts to Monica yesterday. I sure hope she likes them," Kat said, skepticism ringing in her voice.

"There's no doubt, dear. She's going to love them," he comforted.

"Are you going to be able to join us?" she asked.

"I don't know. I've got to leave the hospital sometime today. If I get back in time, I'll come over if you want me to."

"Thanks, Logan. I do. I'm new at this and I'll need all the help I can get," Kat revealed.

"Kat, you're more nervous than if you were performing emergency surgery. Just relax. Everything is going to be fine."

"Okay, I'll try. By the way, what's taking you away from the hospital on Christmas Eve?"

"Well, I didn't want to tell you until I got back, but I've got to go down to the State Welfare Department. Mr. Phillips said they have a family ready to take Tiffany. I insisted on meeting them. I wanted to do it after Christmas, but they want to come and meet her tomorrow. It's sort of like a Christmas present for her. So, I agreed to meet them today."

Logan could see the wind go out of Kat's sails. She tried unsuccessfully to cover her obvious disappointment when she said, "That is good news. You're sure you will get to meet the family?"

"I think so. They've told me a little about them, but they won't tell me their name," he tried to explain. Seeing the pain on her face, he added, "Hey, let's not allow that to ruin a perfect day. After all, it is Christmas Eve. Besides, I've got another surprise planned for you when we get home."

Her thoughts elsewhere, Kat dismissed Logan's words as they pulled into the hospital parking lot and she gathered her stuff from the car. Just inside the hospital door, he remembered, "I forgot some papers on the Hutchinson matter in the car. I've got to go back and get them. I'll see you later. Good luck." Kissing her on her cheek, he turned and headed back to the car. After he reopened the door, he slipped behind the wheel. Checking over his shoulder to make sure she wasn't watching, he started the car and left the hospital parking lot.

The hospital was especially festive that day. Everyone was looking forward to their own celebrations when work was done. Quiet little departmental parties were being held everywhere. But that didn't alleviate Kat's apprehension. She had tried not thinking about it, but that didn't work either. So, she tried to lose herself in her work. While others partied, she conducted her daily routine of reports and rounds, finishing with Noel.

As soon as she walked into his room, he could see the nervousness in her eyes, so he asked, "Something the matter, Dr. Stone?"

"Is it that obvious?"

"I'm afraid it is."

"I'm trying to cover it up, but it's just that I've never done anything like this before. I've never tried to make a little girl happy—especially at Christmas time. I don't even know what kids like," she confessed.

"Well then, it's time you learned. You can't go through life without making at least one child happy. Besides, I've got a hunch it's going to come naturally once you get started," he smiled.

"You definitely have more faith than I do, Noel, but that isn't a new revelation, now is it?"

"You have more than you think, Dr. Stone."

"Yeah, well maybe, but before I go over to peds, I've got to check you out. How are you feeling?" she inquired, trying to fulfill her doctorly duties.

"Last night was a better night. Some of the nausea has passed, but the pain is still there and I get tired very quickly. It seems like I've lost all of my strength."

"That's understandable. Let's not forget you're still a very sick man, and as soon as Christmas is over we're going to start radiation treatments," Kat warned, not wanting Noel to forget the seriousness of his condition.

"I know, I know, but that's not going to stop me from enjoying tonight and tomorrow," he exerted.

Kat felt a special bond which had grown between the two of them over the past couple of weeks and she liked what she felt. It was something that had been missing in her life for a long, long time, making her want to savor it forever. Seeing the love in his eyes, she asked, "Do you still feel up to helping me with Tiffany today?"

"Even as weak as I am, a pack of wild horses couldn't keep me away from this one," he explained.

"Good, but I've got to make a couple of stops first. I'll be back to get you in an hour or so and we'll go over to pediatrics with Tiff."

"I'll be ready."

Walking out of the pleasant room, Kat thought to herself, "I'll bet you will, Noel. I'll bet you will."

Just outside, she was met by Sarah, who had been looking for her. "Dr. Stone, could you come down to the ER for a minute?"

"Is there something wrong, Sarah?"

"No. It's just a shift change, but we've planned a little party before everyone leaves for Christmas and we wanted you to come," Sarah explained, having drawn the unpleasant lot of inviting her.

"In that case, I'll come right down, but I've only got a minute. I've made arrangements to take little Tiffany over to pediatrics for Santa's visit."

Sarah smiled with newfound respect for her boss, as they walked together into the ER. The chatter of happy people wishing each other Merry Christmas and Happy Holidays immediately engulfed them. Phil was in an especially festive spirit. Producing a little sprig of mistletoe, he held it above Sarah's head, bent over, and kissed her as everyone laughed.

Looking directly at Phil after his escapade, Dr. Stone asked in her typically stern manner, "Phil, give it to me."

"Oh, Dr. Stone, it's Christmas Eve. Can't I have a little fun on Christmas Eve?" he pleaded for clemency.

"Just give it to me, Phil," she repeated, holding out her hand.

Thinking she had changed her opinion of Dr. Stone too quickly, Sarah was more surprised than anyone when Kat took the sprig of mistletoe, held it above Phil's head, gave him a holiday peck on the cheek, and said, "Merry Christmas, Phil, and the best for the new year."

Standing back away from the flushed face of the startled orderly, an ovation of cheers erupted from the other members of the ER staff. Milling around with all of the employees, Kat felt a closeness with her co-workers she had never felt before and it brought a bright smile to her face. Drinking a bit of egg nog and having a slice of pumpkin bread, she laughed as they all sang "We Wish You a Merry Christmas." Glancing at the clock on the wall, she knew it was time to take Tiffany up to see Santa. So, reluctantly, she excused herself from the festivities and moved down the hall to the burn unit and Tiffany's room. Trailing behind her, Phil spoke up, "I'd love to wheel her over for you, Dr. Stone, if it's all right?"

"Sure, Phil. I'll need some help. I've got to stop and get Mr. Trudeau. He's going to go with us. So, if you can manage Tiff's gurney, I'll push him in a wheel-chair."

Smiling in agreement, Phil followed Kat into the small child's room.

"Hey, Kiddo! Are you ready to go see Santa?" Kat asked.

A small whisper-like voice answered, "Not really, I'm scared. What if he doesn't like me all bandaged up?"

In a big, bold voice, Phil belted out, "It's all right, Tiff. There's nothing frightening about this. Dr. Stone will be with you and she's the best."

Grinning her thanks, Kat moved over to the bed, picked up the little wrapped hand, and promised, "You'll have a great time, Tiff. There will be presents, treats, and songs. And I've asked a friend of yours to come along."

"Who, Dr. Kat?" she anxiously asked.

"Mr. Trudeau. He said yes and he's been waiting for you all day. We need to go pick him up on the way. Do you think we should go?"

"Oh yes, Dr. Kat. I wanna see Grandpa Trudeau again," she squealed in excitement.

"Then we'd better get going. Move her out, Phil," Kat commanded like a trail boss.

Pushing her out of the glass cubicle, everyone called out their best wishes as she passed through the

ER on her way up to the children's party. Picking up Noel along the way, they finally arrived in pediatrics where they found the party already underway. Nurses and doctors, mommies and daddies, were all gathered around various bedsides, laughing and having fun. Some of the children were up and walking, while others were in wheelchairs. A group of children still in bed, like Tiffany, were gathered against the wall.

As Phil pushed Tiffany into the large room, Monica, the head nurse of pediatrics, walked over and asked, "Well. This must be Tiffany, right?"

Nodding her bandaged little head just a tiny bit, Tiffany smiled a faint smile at being recognized. Although she and Kat were both afraid in their own way, it didn't take long before they were all singing "Jingle Bells" and other children's carols. With Kat holding one of Tiffany's hands and Noel holding the other, they belted out the words they knew to each song.

Standing in the background, having slipped in behind them, Logan watched as happiness and joy flowed uninhibited from his wife. Content to just observe, he decided not to intercede. So, he just stood back filled with love, watching his wife.

Finishing the final chorus of "Up on the Housetop," Monica stopped the applause and announced, "I've just heard that someone special is in the hospital and if we listen really hard, maybe we can hear his sleigh bells."

Instantly, the entire room fell silent, as each child strained to hear the faintest sound of tinkling bells. Not hearing anything, Monica added, "Maybe we should call him with a song. Let's all sing 'Here Comes Santa Claus.' If he hears it, then maybe he'll come." Raising her hands and motioning to Karen sitting at the piano, everyone started singing.

In the middle of the song, the chiming of sleigh bells could be heard echoing down the hall as Santa came into the pediatrics ward on a dead run, hollering, "Ho! Ho! Ho! Merry Christmas, boys and girls! Merry Christmas!"

The wide-eyed excitement of each child was no more evident than in the beautiful blue eyes of little Tiffany Welch. Open as large as she could force them, her little bandaged hands squeezed as tight as they were able to squeeze, against Dr. Kat's and Grandpa Noel's hands.

Standing beside Tiffany's raised bed, Kat felt the moisture of a tear as it unexpectedly rolled down her cheek. Letting go of Tiffany's hand, Noel wheeled himself around to the other side of the bed. Having watched Kat's joy overflow, he stood up beside her and said, "You see, Dr. Stone, how the happiness of others fills your own heart with joy? Tiffany fits right in, even though her scars are deep. What you have done for her today will remain with her forever as a bright spot in an otherwise disastrous holiday."

Looking straight into those dark brown eyes of the elderly man, Kat smiled and threw her arms around his neck, and cried, "Thank you, Noel. If it wasn't for you, I would never have experienced what I am feeling today."

As she was revealing her feelings to Noel, she saw Logan standing in the background. Smiling a devoted smile, she took her arms from around Noel's neck, wiped the tears from her eyes, moved over to her husband, and said, "Oh, Logan, I'm so glad you came. Do you see the happiness? Do you see the joy in her eyes? Isn't it great?"

Catching her in an embrace, he knew that even if he hadn't seen the joy and happiness in the eyes of Tiffany Welch, he could sure see it in the eyes of his wife. He had never seen them gleam with so much exhilaration. But before he could answer, Kat had him by the arm and was dragging him over to Tiffany's bed.

Just after they arrived, Tiffany got another visitor. Bouncing over to her side, the jolly old elf laughed, "Ho! Ho! Ho! Look who's here. You're Tiffany, aren't you?"

Nodding her head in almost disbelief at being this close to Santa Claus, she couldn't speak. But that was okay because Santa spoke for both of them.

"I think I have something here in my bag for you. I know you've been a good little girl this year and do you know what Santa does when kids have been good?"

Again her bandaged little head nodded up and down. Having received the acknowledgment he wanted, he reached into the big, red, velvet bag he was carrying and pulled out a large, wrapped gift. Handing it to Tiffany, he said, "Merry Christmas, little one."

Squeezing tightly on her husband's arm, tears flooded Kat's eyes as Santa moved on to another child. Not wanting to interrupt Kat's moment with her husband, Noel bent over and helped Tiffany unwrap the gift. Once more, Tiffany's swollen little eyes bulged with excitement and joy as she opened her present. Inside the box she found a new dress, some books, and an electronic toy game. Fumbling with her bandaged hands, she picked each item up with difficulty and held them as she said, "Look, Dr. Kat. Look what Santa gave me."

Bending over the bed, Kat hugged the little girl and said, "How wonderful! You deserve it, Tiff. You deserve it."

Santa eventually finished with all of the children in the ward before he made his exit. Everyone was thrilled with what they received and showed off whatever it was to their guests. Kat enthusiastically watched Tiffany try to play with her electronic toy. She could see her tiring, so she decided to take Tiffany back to her cubicle and have Logan drop an exhausted Noel off in his room. As she positioned Tiffany's bed back in her small room, she asked, "Did you have a good time, Tiff?"

"Oh yes, Dr. Kat. I've never been to a party like that before. I was so excited to see Santa. I've never been that close to him before."

Saddened to learn she had never before met Santa Claus, Kat smiled and comforted, "Well, now you've met him and I'm sure you won't forget. Nor will he ever forget."

"No, I won't ever forget, Dr. Kat. It was awesome."

"Tiff, it's time to get some rest. You've had a full day and too much excitement is not good for a little girl in your condition. So try to relax. You need to get some sleep. Before I leave, I will give you some medication that will help."

"Oh, Dr. Kat. This is the best Christmas I've ever had."

Feeling a wealth of deep emotions, Kat added, "Me too, sweetheart. Me too."

Chapter 16

Completely immersed in the new fervor of charity she had discovered, Kat found it difficult to leave Tiffany. After she gave her the medication, she watched until the tiny girl fell asleep. But then, at the urging of her husband, she bade a final Merry Christmas to the slumbering child with a small kiss on her cheek.

Once she was surrounded by the privacy of her own automobile, she lay back against the heated leather seat and collapsed from emotional fatigue. Fondly looking over at her husband behind the steering wheel, she sighed, "I learned something about myself today."

A bit surprised, Logan asked, "And what was that?"

Waxing philosophical in her relaxation, she said, "I learned that you can't really find yourself, until you lose yourself."

Logan listened intently, but was confused with her revelation and replied, "That sounds somewhat contradictory to me."

"Not really. You see, ever since my mother died I've been all alone. I never had an example of someone who wanted more for me than they wanted for themselves. Consequently, everything I got, I got because I earned it or stole it. When things started falling apart with Tiffany, I felt lost. You kept telling me not to lose hope, but for me there was no hope because I wasn't in control. The more the situation slipped out of my control, the deeper my feelings of being lost became. However, all of that has changed. Today I found out that there is a much greater power than I possess. I learned that I could only draw on that power when I stopped worrying about myself and completely focused my attention on making someone else happy," she enlightened. A contented smile spread all over her face.

"I must admit, Miss Tiffany Welch has brought about a change in you."

Brightening even more at the mention of the little girl's name, Kat radiated, "Oh, Logan, did you see her? Her eyes were as big as saucers the whole afternoon. You could see her beaming clear through her bandages. I never knew something so simple could bring so much happiness and pleasure to anyone. Watching her today showed me how you can forget all about your pain when you have a chance to help someone else embrace happiness."

Sensing the meaning conveyed by her words brought an internal warmth to Logan and he wanted to share in the experience. So, he paid tribute to Kat and said, "Don't forget, most of her joy surfaced, in large part, because of you. If you hadn't come up with that great idea of taking her over to be with the other kids today, she wouldn't have felt all of that enjoyment. She would have just laid in that lonely bed thinking about how miserable her life is."

"But that's what I mean, Logan. When I came up with the idea, I wasn't thinking of myself and what a great plan I came up with. I was thinking of Tiffany. In fact, personally, I was scared. I was so afraid it wouldn't work out. I've been on the edge of my seat now for two days, hoping she would just be able to enjoy herself for a few minutes. It was hard for me, but deep down inside, I think I knew there was no way to force that kind of happiness either. So, I just focused my thoughts on one thing. Help Tiffany have fun. And it succeeded beyond my wildest dreams. But that's not all. I felt a gratification today beyond anything I have ever felt before. In return for my efforts, I felt a calming peace I have never before known."

Pleased by Kat's inner serenity spilling over and filling their restricted surroundings, he longed for their intimate discussion to continue. But these topics automatically shifted when they exited the automobile and went out into the cold night air.

Logan quickly moved in front of his wife in order to open the door for her. He turned the key in the lock and stood back, having pushed the door wide open for her to enter.

Once inside the door and standing in the entryway, she was startled by what she saw and fumbled for words. "Oh, Logan! It's beautiful. Where did that come from?" she asked, overflowing with excitement as she stared at the lovely decorated Christmas tree.

"Surprise! I've been saving this all day. I thought that since this has been such a difficult Christmas, and we aren't going on vacation like we normally do at Christmas, it would be nice to enjoy our first Christmas tree together."

Not hearing the details of his explanation, because she was walking around the tree inspecting each and every decoration, Kat bubbled with newfound festivity.

Overcome by the rising rapture, Logan stifled an emotional cough and reached into his pocket and pulled out an envelope. "That's not all. I've got something else for you, dear."

"Not yet, Logan. I just want to feast on this for the time being. I'm so happy I could burst. Just let me ponder this. I can't even remember the last time I had a Christmas tree in my house. It must have been when I was at the halfway house in high school. You know, I couldn't be bothered with one in college. It never seemed important to me, but after seeing this tree, I'm sure I have been wrong all these years."

"It is beautiful, isn't it?"

"It surely is," she said as she moved and nestled next to her husband.

"I also bought some Christmas music. Do you want me to put it on?"

"Not yet. I have another idea. Let's walk down to the nativity on the corner first. It'll give me a chance to say thanks for such a wonderful day," she persuasively pleaded, tugging on his sleeve.

Seeing the humble desire that bubbled in her eyes, he agreed, took her by the arm, and led her out of their home. Arm in arm, they strolled down to the corner and the unmistakable glow of the nativity. In front of the sacred scene, the loving couple stood while Kat meditated her newfound faith. As they stood in reverence, a light snow began to fall.

Pondering in reserved silence, their quiet reverie was splintered by the shrill chiming of Kat's mobile telephone.

"Did you bring that thing?"

Not answering him, she dug into her pocket, pulled out the ringing phone, flipped the mouth flap down with one motion and then pressed a button as she said, "Dr. Stone speaking . . . I'll be there as soon as I can. And Dan, you've got to keep him breathing until I get there."

Without hesitation, she turned and began running back to the garage as she called back to her husband, "I've got to get to the hospital, stat!"

Disappointed with the unexpected turn of events, his words trailed after her, "Couldn't someone else handle it? It's Christmas Eve."

"Noooo! Something's happened to Noel!" she shouted in reply.

Dropping his shoulders, he headed back to their home. Almost there, he decided to drive down to the hospital to support his wife.

❦

Running straight from the parking lot, Kat entered the medical center in full stride. Not waiting for the elevator, she hit the stairs taking them two at a time. Bursting from the stairwell like an explosion, she glided into room 1225 out of breath. Concentrating on the body lying in the bed, Dr. Anderson and the three nurses failed to notice her entrance. Pushing her way through, she charged, "What's wrong, Dan?"

Dr. Anderson looked and responded, "He can't breathe; his lungs are filled with fluid."

"Where's it coming from? I checked him earlier today and didn't hear anything," she asked.

"I don't know, but I'd guess it's a by-product of the chemo."

"Don't guess, Dan! We need to know for sure," she snapped, fear surrounding each word as she clipped them.

"You're not talking to a medical school student, Kat. You know as well as I do that pneumonia can set in at any time with a patient on chemo," he shouted back, in no mood to accept Kat's domination. Acknowledging her mistake, she was about to try and calm her agitated colleague when the heart monitor connected to Noel Trudeau sounded its recognizable monotone wail.

"Dana, get a crash cart, stat!" Kat called out while beginning CPR, pounding on his heart frantically as she tried to restart the motionless heart.

Grabbing the paddles as quickly as Dana had them prepared, she called out, "Clear!" The body rumbled as the electric shock ripped through its tissue.

When the failed heart didn't respond, she shouted, "Again! Clear!" Noel's lifeless body bounced once again upon the hospital bed without response.

Watching the straight flat line of the heart monitor refuse to change, Kat called, "Give me an 80-milligram epinephrine push, stat." Within seconds the filled syringe was smacked into the distraught doctor's hand. Driving the long, pointed needle into the exposed vein, Kat released the medication with a quick, steady plunge. She picked up the paddles again and adjusted the power. Readying them one more time, Kat called out, "Clear!" Following the electronically forced response to the third shock, the body remained lifeless, accompanied by the straight, flat line on the monitor. With her options disappearing fast, she yelled, "I'm going to open him up. Swathe him with iodine and get me a scalpel, stat." The sterile, stainless steel tool was slapped into her hand as Dana washed the exposed chest with iodine. Carefully, she cut open the lifeless chest of her dear friend. Calling for a rib spreader, she exposed his still heart. Tenderly taking the tired organ into her hand, she began a slow, steady, manual massage of the delicate muscle as she called out, "Don't die, Noel! Please don't die. You can make it!" But the flat line continued to stream across the screen without any change.

Watching the futile attempts of his desperate colleague, Dan Anderson stepped in to express what was obvious to everyone but Katarina.

"Kat, it's no use. He's gone."

Snapping back instantly, she screamed with venom, "It's not your call, Dan! I'm not going to let him die."

Stung by her rebuke, but knowing the uselessness of her efforts, he waited another two minutes, and then reiterated his plea, "Kat! It's over. He's gone."

About to tear his head off, Kat felt Logan's strong hands as they grasped her shoulders.

Leaning forward, he grieved, "Kat, Dan's right. Noel's gone and you can't bring him back. Give it up now."

Feeling her entire strength drain from her body, she uncoiled her hands from around the lifeless heart in the open chest with utmost precision. In tears, she ripped the bloodied latex gloves off of her hands, turned, and collapsed into the secure arms of her comforting husband.

Moments later she twisted, driven by enraged emotions and beat on Logan's chest crying, "It's not fair, Logan. It's just not fair. Why did he have to die tonight? Of all nights, why tonight?"

With his arms encircled around his wife, he tried to comfort her, but his words rang hollow, "I don't know, Kat. I don't know."

The frenzied activity had now been replaced with an unusually serene silence, as Kat's physical rampage withered and left her to deteriorate into uncontrollable sobs. The staccato silence was broken when the orderlies came to take Noel's deceased body out of his room. Cleaning up behind them, Julie began to gather the few items Noel had scattered around the bed. She reached down to pick up the individual pieces of the old nativity and noticed a piece of paper with writing on it, awkwardly stuck under the manger. Pulling it out, the bold lettering **Doctor Katarina Stone** screamed out to her.

Turning around to find Dr. Stone, but not wanting to interrupt the tender moment between husband and wife, she patiently waited for it to end. Falling back to the unenviable task of gathering additional articles, something prompted her to speak.

This time she called out, "Dr. Stone, I think this is for you."

Steadied by Logan's arms, Kat turned and took the note from Julie. She opened the folded pages and read the letter out loud through her tears.

Dear Dr. Stone,

If you are reading this note, then my pre-monitions from this afternoon have proven true and I have left this life to go meet my dear mate, Maria. Although my life is over, there is still something I want to tell you. In the last few days, you have given an old man much joy. I felt emotions I never thought I would feel again.

Watching you today with Tiffany was one of the happiest days I can remember. The pure love of Christ was present wherever I turned. I saw in you a new person. A person full of love and compassion. A person who found herself in the love of a child.

Remember, Dr. Stone, it is Christ's birth, life, death, and resurrection that are most important. The events of today displayed what can happen when you invite Him in and let His love guide your actions.

I know that when I pass to the other side in a few short minutes, He will be waiting alongside my sweet Maria with open arms.

My dear Dr. Stone, let Him in. Let Him into your life forever.

Now, I don't have much to leave behind, but I want to give you what I cherish most. It may not seem like much to you yet, but it was my most cherished earthly possession, my nativity. It was Mama's. It brought a miracle to us during the war and it has provided much inspiration to me since.

As you can tell, it is worn, but it is worn with love. Each piece carries special memories for me and I hope they will for you. I'm getting very weak and it's getting harder and harder to breathe, but I have one last request. Give the Christ child to Tiffany. Tell her it's from Grandpa Noel and let her know Christ will watch over her precious life.

But remember, Dr. Stone, above all else, that you knew someone who knew Christ. He lives! He is my Savior and my Redeemer and more importantly now, He is yours as well.

Cherish the joy of life, but always remember its source. It comes from Him.

Lovingly, your friend,
Noel

Tears dotted the page as they fell from Kat's swollen eyes. Walking over to the nativity, she picked up the Christ child and clutched it close to her breast. Amid a new surge of unrestrained emotions, she turned back to her husband and whimpered, "Logan, please gather the other pieces of the nativity and bring them down to Tiffany's room with me."

Following behind her, he squeezed the worn pieces of olive wood so they wouldn't fall and moved into the silent cubicle with his wife.

The faint strains of Christmas music trickled into the isolated room, giving a backdrop to the grieving couple. The small, bandaged child rustled from the noise of their entrance, but did not awaken. Setting the mixed up pieces down quietly, Logan comforted Kat by putting his arm around her and giving her a gentle squeeze. Nestling closer to his body, she managed to say amid her sobs, "Why does he want me to keep the nativity, when he wants Tiffany to have the Christ child . . . ?"

Unable to finish her thought because of overpowering grief, she paused, trying to collect her jumbled thoughts and then continued, almost confused, "I don't understand. It seems so senseless to break up the pieces, especially after all the years it was in Noel's family, through the war and all."

Before she could speak again, Logan reached into his pocket and pulled out the envelope he tried to give her earlier at home. Turning his wife so he could look straight into her grief-stricken eyes, his sentiment began to overflow, when he cried, "It's not senseless, Kat. It was meant to be. Noel was a very wise old man and he must have known the solution to this dilemma."

Pausing so he could wipe the tears from his eyes, he held up the envelope. Opening it, he withdrew the enclosed papers. Holding tightly onto his wife, he revealed, "Kat! I have something for you. I made arrangements with the state for you and me to adopt your little Tiffany. It is all taken care of except for our signatures. Noel must have known in his heart that we were meant to be together. That's why he separated the pieces, knowing shortly they would be joined together again."

Throwing her arms around her husband's neck in stunned astonishment, her tears flowed freely as she clutched him. Unable to speak, the two just clung to each other. The Christmas music in the background seemed to rise in volume and the words of the humble carol filled the air.

"Noel, Noel, Noel, Noel. Born is the King of Israel!"

Epilogue

It was cold. In fact, it was too cold. The big lake was living up to its reputation and the soft, fluffy, white flakes of snow falling heavily from the sky didn't temper its fury one bit. It had been a while since the homes surrounding Lake Michigan had been battered by such a storm. It seemed to have everyone holed up. Everyone, that is, except an excited Stone family who had a love of December snowstorms.

Logan had started a fire when he climbed out of bed first thing in the morning, trying to initiate the ambience of the holiday season. The warm fire succored the comfortable home as he sat at the kitchen table finishing the last bites of hot cakes smothered in maple syrup, bacon strips, and hot cocoa.

Just off to the side of the kitchen table, Kat and Tiffany worked their way through a maze of tangled Christmas lights and decorations, which had been pulled out from under the stairway earlier in the morning. On the stove, a potpourri of cinnamon and cloves simmered and Christmas carols played on the stereo in the background.

Tiffany carefully pulled each piece of an old, worn nativity out from a secure box. After she had fully inspected it, she handed it to her mother who arranged it on the kitchen table. Together, they took each piece and walked into the living room where they placed them in perfect spacing on a Queen Anne table covered with angel hair next to the fireplace.

Calling to Logan in the other room to come and join them, they asked him to retrieve the final piece, a worn, cherubic Christ child laying in a manger. Once in the living room, they shared a joyous memory. Then the Christ child was given to Tiffany to place the precious piece amidst the other hallowed figures.

Stepping back to join her parents, her mother, Kat, sighed, "Perfect!" Just then, over the speaker system of their stereo, the words to a sacred carol boomed,

The first Noel the angels did say
Was to certain poor shepherds
In fields where they lay.
In fields where they, lay keeping their sheep
On a cold winter's night that was so deep.
Noel, Noel, Noel, Noel.
Born is the king of Israel!

About the Author

As a public speaker, Phil can be heard in cities through-out the world. He has traveled extensively and lived in several different countries, developing a knowledge of various family and cultural traditions. He combines that knowledge with his own love of Christmas to bring us *Noel's Miracle*. Phil and his wife Mollie have four children and reside in Lehi, Utah.